WHEN EMMALYNN REMEMBERS

Her journey into the past threatens to destroy her future...

The blood of old Henrietta Stern still stains the veranda of the dilapidated seaside mansion she willed to her lovely young companion. But Emmalynn Rogers has completely blocked out the horror of the murder she witnessed.

What will happen when Emmalynn remembers?

The accused murderer died in jail, but George Reed will stop at nothing to clear his father's name.

What will happen when Emmalynn remembers?

Only two people know the identity of the killer: the girl whose fear and terror have buried it deep within her subconscious...and someone very close to her, ready to kill again the moment Emmalynn remembers...

WHEN EMMALYNN REMEMBERS

When Emmalynn Remembers

by
Jennifer Wilde

MAGNA PRINT BOOKS
Long Preston, North Yorkshire,
England.

British Library Cataloguing in Publication Data.

Wilde, Jennifer
 When Emmalynn remembers.
 I. Title
 813.54

ISBN 0-7505-0136-7
ISBN 0-7505-0137-5 pbk

First Published in Great Britain 1991

Copyright © 1970 by T.E. Huff

Published in Large Print 1991 by arrangement with Severn House Publishers Ltd., London

All rights reserved. No part of this publication may be reproduced, stored in a retrieval system, or transmitted in any form or by any means, electronic, mechanical, photocopying, recording or otherwise, without the prior permission of the Copyright owner.

Printed and bound in Great Britain by
T.J. Press (Padstow) Ltd., Cornwall, PL28 8RW.

CHAPTER ONE

I got off the bus with a weary sigh and stood on the corner as it vanished into the fog, a huge red monster soon swallowed up by the blue-grey swirls. It was Friday night, and I looked forward to a long, restful weekend. Clive had given me a sheaf of photographs to study, hoping I might select a few I thought good enough for the book. I had been working for Clive just four months now, and already I was a full-fledged assistant. Although I never touched a camera or, Heaven forbid, one of the expensive lights, I brought him coffee and sandwiches, pacified his temperamental models, saw that his supplies were properly stocked, ran errands and, ultimately, did everything necessary to keep Courtney Studios from sprawling into chaos. His New York publishers were pressuring him about the book of photographs now, and for the past two weeks the studio had been a madhouse, Clive scouring the streets of London for unique and unusual shots and his faithful assistant fighting off hordes of creditors who threatened to demolish the place if the bills weren't promptly paid.

But this weekend I could rest. Clive was taking a trip down the Thames on a coal barge, hoping to get enough material to complete the photographic essay on London life, and I intended to forget the wild, wonderful confusion of the studio and simply relax. I would pick out a few of the photographs I thought he liked best, but the rest of the time I would spend in luxurious idleness. I would lounge in bed till noon, wash my hair, read a new novel and, if worse came to worse, watch television.

Billie would be there, of course, but Billie and I never got in each other's way. We shared the flat in Chelsea with perfect harmony, each respecting the other's privacy when privacy was the mood of the moment. There would undoubtedly be a slew of gentlemen callers, but Billie would see that they stayed in the living room and demolished as little furniture as possible. Unless there were at least three or four men fighting over her, Billie felt she was a failure as a woman, and her gallants ranged from a member of Parliament to the bus boy at our favourite restaurant.

After so many years of dreary existence as paid companion to a haughty old dowager, I welcomed the riotous colour Clive and Billie brought into my life. There were times, though, when I longed for a less frantic pace, and this weekend was going to be one of those times. As I walked along the wet sidewalk now I revelled in the thought of forty-eight hours of seclusion. It was going to be glorious.

It was cold and damp tonight, and I pulled my coat collar up around my ears. Although the fog was thick, the neon lights burned brightly, red and blue, gold and green, glowing mistily through the fog and reflecting on the wet sidewalks. The streets were as crowded and noisy as ever, a carnival of sight and sound that never ceased. A crowd of teenagers spilled boisterously into a dance hall across the way. A stout woman in tweeds walked a pair of yapping terriers. I passed a surly blond giant in boots and black leather jacket, his long curls falling in a tangle about his shoulders, his eyes hidden by a pair of dark glasses. A thin-faced brunette in purple miniskirt and orange stockings hurried after him, her high heels tapping angrily on the pavement. A pop band was blaring in the dance hall, people shouted and cheered, and, as always, the roar and screech of traffic was deafening. I was accustomed to this noise and paid very little attention to it. I sometimes wondered how I had ever been able to endure the dim, murky silence of resort hotels out of season and watering places long since deserted by any fashionable clientele.

I loved London, and I loved my new life. As I stepped into the hall of our apartment building, I had not the slightest inkling that all this colour and furore was about to end.

As I walked towards the stairs, Mrs Craigston approached me. She was our landlady, a plump, grizzled old woman who wore felt slippers and soiled print dresses. Her flat was on the lower floor, and her door always stood open so that she could observe anyone who stepped into the building. Mrs Craigston frequently told Billie that she ran a respectable house and would not tolerate all these men swarming up and down the stairs at all hours of the night, but in truth she tolerated everything but unpaid rent. If rent wasn't paid on the day it was due she became a veritable fury, hounding her victim until he either paid or contemplated murder or suicide or both. Billie and I were always prompt with our rent money and, consequently, could have kept a troop of trained seals in our room without risking anything but a lashing from Mrs Craigston's virulent tongue. I rather liked the old creature, but Billie swore she was a retired white slaver who kept a hypodermic in her top desk drawer just in case the apartment house stopped paying enough profit.

Mrs Craigston shuffled towards me, her felt slippers flopping on the shabby carpet. Her grey hair was in curlers, and she gripped a sandwich in her hand as though she feared I would snatch it away from her.

'There's men in your flat,' she said.

'Oh?'

'Yep, funny lookin' men. Not the *usual* kind—' She paused to let this comment sink in. 'These are wearin' suits and have haircuts. They come in 'bout an hour ago and asked for Miss Emmalynn Rogers, lookin' grim and up to no good. One of 'em said he was a doctor—' She paused again to study my waistline for any telling bulk. 'And the other was a lawyer. You ain't—uh—ain't in any *trouble* are you?'

'Not that I know of—'

'Well, I'm makin' myself clear here 'n now. I ain't havin' any of it, not a bit. It's bad enough to have them artists 'n undertakers 'n actors stormin' in to see Miss Billie at all hours, but when doctors and lawyers start comin' to a perfectly respectable house, I intend to make myself heard. You just remember that—'

'Thank you, Mrs Craigston,' I said politely.

'I mean every word of it, Miss Em'lynn. And furthermore, Miss Billie owes me two pounds for that rubber tree plant her actor friend took out last week to hock. He thought I didn't see 'im creepin' by with his coat wrapped around it. I saw 'im all right. Why, the pot alone was worth—'

'I'll tell her.' I promised.

I hurried on up the stairs, anxious to avoid one of her interminable tirades. I could smell cooked cabbage and ale, an odour that hung over the place like incense, and I heard a couple on the second landing quarrelling. Mrs Craigston's was not the last word in elegance, but it was semi-respectable, conveniently located and, most important, all Billie and I could afford. The wallpaper on our landing was hideous, faded pink roses against a light green background, and naked light bulbs burned dimly in branches of tortured brass sconces on either side of our door.

I could hear voices in the living room as I stepped into the foyer. I took off my coat and hung it on the clothes rack, then paused in front of the murky full length mirror and inspected myself. My long auburn hair was windblown and my cheeks were a little flushed. My lids were shadowed with faint grey smudges, the result of overwork, but the dark blue eyes sparkled with curiosity. I knew very well who the doctor was, but I wondered why on earth a lawyer should be calling with him. I straightened the skirt of my dark green dress, smoothed my hair and stepped into the living room.

Doctor Peter Clarkson stepped forward to greet me. He was fifty-three, a handsome man with silver hair, a ruddy complexion and the shoulders of a soccer star. He wore a sportscoat of black and grey plaid and florid tie of pink and orange silk. His blue eyes twinkled mischievously behind his heavy black horn-rimmed glasses, and his hand crushed mine as I submitted it to be shaken.

'You're looking glorious, Emmalynn,' he shouted. Dr Clarkson did not really shout, but his voice was so loud and booming that it always sounded like he was keeping score at a cricket match. 'Fine, fine! Much better than last time I saw you. Clive must be keeping you in shape.'

Clive Courtney was Dr Clarkson's nephew, and it was Dr Clarkson who had introduced me to the photographer and obtained the job for me. I owed a lot to this rough-mannered, robust man, and I felt a great affection for him as he stood back now to examine me more thoroughly.

'I swear,' he said, 'if I were twenty years younger—no, ten!—I'd sweep you off your feet. A raving beauty! If I didn't know my nephew so well, I'd be worried about you—'

'There's no danger,' I said.

Clive Courtney was well on his way to becoming one of the most famous photographers in London, and he was adorable, dedicated to his work and a charming man, but he was not particularly interested in women, at least not in any way that would jeopardize the virtue of any woman who worked around him. He was as safe as houses, Billie claimed, a little put out that he didn't try to woo her when she went to pose for him.

I looked over Dr Clarkson's shoulder at the man who stood by the window. He was tall and thin, wearing a severe black suit and a drab grey tie. His face was angular and bony, his eyes an icy blue, and his thin brown hair was slicked down flat against his skull. His was the kind of face that caused small children to clutch their mothers' skirts, and I felt a slight chill myself as his cold blue eyes swept over me.

'May I introduce Albert Lock,' Dr Clarkson said. 'Mr Lock has been looking for you for some time. He finally came to me and asked if I knew where you could be located. Of course I brought him here.'

'How do you do, Mr Lock,' I said, sounding much calmer than I felt. Something about Albert Lock's manner caused me to bristle, and it was difficult to keep from showing it.

'Miss Rogers,' he replied, nodding briefly.

'I suppose you want to know what this is all about?' the doctor said. He shrugged his massive shoulders and frowned a little. 'It—it took me a while to decide whether or not this was—best for you, Emmalynn. Mr Lock is a lawyer, and he has some interesting news, but I'm a doctor and you're my patient—pardon, *were* my patient—and I was dubious at first. However, I can assure you I don't believe this will—harm you. In any way. You're perfectly capable of handling it.'

'I'm not an invalid,' I said, rather irritably, 'nor am I insane. I am perfectly normal and capable of—'

'Hold on now,' Dr Clarkson protested. He grinned. 'She has a temper to go with that red hair, Lock. Of course you're normal, Emmalynn, and no one's trying to say you're not. Yours is an unusual case—'

'Perhaps you should clarify just exactly what her case is,' Lock said in a frigid tone. 'My client isn't quite sure, and I'm not certain that I understand fully myself. If there is any illness—'

Dr Clarkson scowled, showing his dislike of the lawyer. 'Emmalynn is suffering from amnesia, Mr Lock. Partial amnesia and, I am sure, temporary amnesia. She had quite a shock the night of—the night it happened. She and

Mrs Stern had quarrelled a couple of days before, and Miss Rogers left the house, left the town, in fact, and came to London. Then she began to feel remorseful and sorry that she had left the old woman alone, and she came back. She came back the night of the crime, and she saw—everything.'

'This wasn't public knowledge,' Lock said promptly.

'Emmalynn was found by Officer Stevens of the Brighton police. She was wandering around in a daze. Stevens is a good friend of mine, and I was at my cottage in Brighton for the weekend. He put her under my care. Emmalynn has been my patient ever since.'

'This amnesia—' Lock began.

'She remembers nothing of the night of the crime. She has blotted it out—completely, so completely that she remembers nothing whatsoever about Brighton. She might never have been there at all.'

'But they were there for several months—'

'True. And those months are a complete blank.'

Lock looked at me as though he were staring at an open grave. I might have been a raving lunatic from the expression on his face. Dr Clarkson saw the look and was extremely irritated by it.

'Emmalynn is a healthy girl, perfectly sound, perfectly sane in every respect. She just doesn't remember a few months. There are times in the life of every man that he would like to forget—Emmalynn has done that. It is that simple.'

'Still,' Lock persisted, 'I find it hard to believe that there was an actual witness to the crime and it never came out at the inquest. This officer Stevens you mentioned—'

'Law and medicine seldom see eye to eye,' Clarkson said irritably. 'In this one case, however, we have an exception. All parties concerned felt Miss Rogers' condition was too grave to risk exposing her to any form of questioning. She was in the hospital, under sedation, for two weeks. Everyone who knew Mrs Stern knew that she had mistreated the girl and that Miss Rogers left Brighton two days before the crime and went to London.'

'Miss Rogers wasn't even mentioned in the newspapers,' Lock said. 'Can you explain that?'

'The newspapers weren't interested in a former paid companion. After all, man, they had a bloody axe murder—one of the goriest in years—and they had the body, the weapon, the murderer. That was enough to keep them occupied for quite some time.'

I had had enough of being discussed as though I was an invisible third party. I went over to the sideboard and poured a gigantic drink, something I seldom did. The gesture was more defiant than sensible, for I gagged on my first swallow and slammed the glass down noisily.

'Look,' I said, 'I come home after a long, hard day, ready to relax and forget all the troubles of the world, and I find—this. Would someone kindly tell me what this is all about, or shall we continue to speculate on whether I shall or shall not go berserk in Hyde Park and massacre innocent bystanders with a switchblade!'

Dr Clarkson grinned at that, and even Albert Lock looked amused. I plopped down on the sofa and suggested that the men might be more comfortable if they sat down, too. Dr Clarkson sprawled out on the end of the sofa and took out his pipe. Lock sat primly on the edge of the only uncomfortable chair in the room. We stared at each other for a moment, I wanted to start screaming, but I knew such an action would be unwise. Lock would no doubt lunge out the door and go tearing down the stairs in horror. He still looked uneasy, as though I might pull a knife at any moment.

'Lock has some news for you,' Dr Clarkson said.

'Ahem,' Lock said.

'Pardon?' I said.

'Ahem,' he cleared his throat again. 'This is all very complicated,' he said. 'Legally, that is. A question of first will and second will and so forth and so forth and probate court and mental state of author at time will was made—I can explain in detail if you prefer.'

'Please don't,' I said, wishing he would suddenly vanish right before my eyes.

'My client, Gordon Stuart, Mrs Stern's younger brother and her only living relative, stood, by rights, to inherit everything from her, and as you probably know, Mrs Stern was quite wealthy—'

'Yes, I seem to recall that,' I retorted.

'Two wills were found. The first did, in fact, leave everything to my client, and the second, which was just this week declared the legitimate will, left everything to him with the exception of the property in Brighton and everything in the house. The latter, Miss Rogers, was left to you. You are now an heiress.'

'I—I don't believe it,' I stammered.

'It's all quite legitimate. The house, all the furnishings, everything in or on the property belongs to you.'

'There,' Dr Clarkson said. 'It's finally out. I thought you'd like to hear it, Emmalynn.

How does it feel to be an heiress?'

'I—you mean she left it to me?'

'Indeed she did,' Lock said. I could tell by the tone of his voice that he was extremely unhappy with the situation. He looked at me as though I might have drugged the old woman and forced her to make a new will.

'But—just a minute,' I said. 'You say Gordon Stuart is your client. If that's so, then what are you doing in my living room?'

Albert Lock smiled. It was a creepy smile, the kind I fancied a vampire might make before sinking its teeth into someone's flesh. 'Mr Stuart has a—shall we say sentimental attachment to the house in Brighton. He is quite fond of the place—'

I shook my head. 'Gordon Stuart never gave a hang about anything that had to do with his family, Mr Lock, and he has never had a sentimental emotion in his life.'

'You've met Mr Stuart?'

'Several times.'

'And you *remember* him?'

'Vividly,' I retorted. 'I was Mrs Stern's companion for seven years, Mr Lock, and I remember six and a half of those years in minute detail. I remember Gordon Stuart, all right, and I'm beginning to wonder why he sent you to see me. He *did* send you?'

'Indeed he did,' Albert Lock said hastily. 'Mr Stuart has authorized me to make you quite a generous offer for the property in Brighton. He'd be pleased to take it off your hands.'

'I'll bet he would,' I snapped. 'Well, he can rot in Hell!'

'Pardon?'

'I said he can rot in Hell. This is—all very sudden, and I'm still not quite sure what it all means, but if Henrietta Stern left me a house in Brighton she must have had a darn good reason for it—'

'I can assure you the house is yours. A clerk will be calling on you tomorrow with some papers you must sign. Once they have your signature the deed will be turned over to you, to do with as you please. My client will be willing to pay—'

'He can go hang,' I said, my voice suddenly polite. 'If it was left to me, Mr Gordon Stuart is not going to get his hands on it. And you can tell him that, Mr Lock. The sooner the better.'

'Miss Rogers—'

'I don't intend to let him have it,' I said firmly.

'Bravo!' Dr Clarkson said.

We both turned to glare at him.

Dr Clarkson fiddled with his pipe and grinned. 'Don't pay any attention to me,' he said. 'I'm just a spectator.' His grin broadened. 'Amnesia or no, Lock, you've got to admit she's got spunk! She may have forgotten some things, but she hasn't forgotten how to fight, and if your Mr Stuart really wants that place in Brighton it looks like he's going to have quite a battle in store for him!'

CHAPTER TWO

Billie Mead was tall and lanky with enormous brown eyes and tawny gold hair that swirled about her shoulders in disorderly locks. Had she really tried, Billie could have been a top professional model, for she had the look, the slouchy walk that was constantly in demand by photographers and fashion editors, but my roommate was one of those rare individuals who didn't seem to care about financial gain. She would rather stay out till all hours crawling from pub to pub with half a dozen merry companions than to go to bed at eight so she would be fresh and photogenic in the morning.

She preferred snatching casual modelling assignments here and there to working eight hours a day with one of the highly prosperous agencies that were always pestering her to sign with them. She was blithe and carefree, a child of nature who delighted in life. She could be incredibly lazy, staying around the place all day, sleeping, painting her toenails, reading the tabloids, soaking in a hot tub, or, if the notion struck her, charged with a frenzied energy that sent her darting from one job to another in quick succession. Despite her reckless and restless philosophy, she was warm, generous and shrewdly intelligent. She had been a great comfort to me during the past months.

She held up a vividly coloured Spanish shawl now, toyed with the fringe and draped it over her shoulder. 'I don't suppose it would be practical for Brighton,' she said, discarding it. She seized a black silk bikini with large white polka dots and stuffed it into her suitcase. 'I don't know if they're ready for my bikinis,' she remarked, taking up another of magenta red and tossing it on top of the other. 'I really don't know what to expect of this trip—but it's going to be glorious just the same!'

'I don't imagine we'll be spending much time on the beach,' I informed her. 'We're only going to be there a few days.'

'But there's a perfectly marvellous beach in front of the house,' Billie protested, 'private, too. I saw it in the pictures of the place they sent you with the deed.'

'It looked rather treacherous to me,' I replied.

'Dearest, water is water and sand is sand, and the sun is bound to be out sometime while we're there. I couldn't hold my head up if I came back without a tan.'

She began to jerk dresses out of the closet and toss them on the bed. They flew through the air like brightly coloured flowers and landed in wild confusion on the bed, limp silken petals. Billie began to examine each one of them for flaws. One would have thought she was going on a European jaunt instead of merely driving to Brighton to inspect an old house.

'This trip is just what I needed—just,' she said. 'Peace and quiet and no men—none. Solitude. I think I'll take that Dostoyevsky thing and finish reading it.'

'You've been trying to read that book ever since I've known you.'

'Well, I've finished the *first* chapter—'

Billie was as excited and enthusiastic as a child. I watched her finish packing, wishing I could feel some of her elation. I had signed the official papers a week and a half ago, and

I dreaded going to see the house now. I had put it off as long as possible, claiming I couldn't leave Clive just yet, but Clive had finally selected all the photographs for the book and left yesterday for Devon where he would toil over the text that was to accompany the pictures. Courtney Studios was closed for three weeks and I had nothing to do. I couldn't put off the trip any longer, and I was relieved that Billie had decided to come along. Her company would make it so much easier.

Billie closed the suitcase and stepped over to the dressing table. She examined the pots and jars and bottles, casually sniffing a perfume, dipping her fingertip in a jar of cream, and, finally, she began to paint her fingernails with a slick cinnamon polish. It was ten o'clock at night, and we planned to leave first thing in the morning.

'Your doctor came by yesterday,' Billie remarked. 'You had gone with Clive to the train station to see him off. I forgot to mention it to you.'

'Did he want anything in particular?' I inquired.

'No—' Billie said, drawing the word out. 'He's quite handsome, Em. So rugged and virile. Shame he's old enough to be my father. He looks more like an athlete than a doctor.

And that voice—'

Billie smiled. She was a gorgeous creature, sensual and warm, and men swarmed around her like bees around the proverbial pot of honey. She treated them with casual disdain, but their admiration was as essential to her as air to breathe. I could imagine how Dr Clarkson had reacted to her. He must have been overwhelmed. Most men were.

'What did he say?' I asked.

'Oh—nothing much—' She was being deliberately evasive.

'Come on, Billie,' I said irritably. 'Don't make me drag the information from you.'

'Well, if you must know, he told me to watch after you. Just that.' She frowned. 'I knew it would make you mad. Just look at your expression! Anyway, that's what he said—so there!'

'I wonder why he would have said such a thing? He told me it wouldn't do me any harm. In fact, he seemed to want me to go. He thinks it might cause me to remember—' I paused, looking away from her.

Billie sighed, very philosophical about the whole thing. 'He told me he was sure you'd remember. Maybe not right at first, but after a day or so you'll see something or hear something that will bring it all back. The shock will be terrific, he said, but you'll be completely cured. Is that why you've been putting this off, Em? Because you're afraid to remember?' Her voice was silken, casual, but I could tell that she was genuinely concerned.

'I don't know, Billie.'

'You don't remember *anything* about Brighton?'

'Absolutely nothing. I remember crossing the Channel after we decided to leave France, and I remember seeing the shores of England—that's all. Everything else is a blank—until the day I woke up in Dr Clarkson's cottage, three days after—it happened. He took me to the hospital and then when he was sure I was all right he got me the job with Clive. I met you, we took this flat—and everything has been marvellous since. I've become a new person—an entirely new person. When I think back on all those years I let Henrietta Stern dictate to me—'

'Dearest, you know one of my absolutely unbreakable rules in never to ask anyone about their past, but—well, actually, I'm dying with curiosity! I simply can't feature you as a paid companion to a dictatorial old woman. I thought paid companions belonged to Victorian novels.' She finished painting her nails and held them up to dry. 'It might do you good to talk about it, Em. What was she like?'

'Impossible,' I said, 'and—I pitied her. I suppose that's why I stayed with her. She was a miserable old woman who needed someone to take care of her, and no one else had the patience to put up with her. She was my mother's best friend, and when my mother died I was just seventeen, all alone and absolutely penniless. Henrietta offered to help me and I was glad enough to accept her offer. Later on I saw what a mistake I'd made, but I never had the heart to leave her, until—'

'Until Brighton,' Billie said.

'That's right. I have no earthly idea what we quarrelled about, but it must have been a tremendous battle if I actually had the guts to leave. She promised she'd take care of me, and—I left her and she died in such a horrible way—'

'Burt Reed must have hated her to have killed her like that,' Billie said.

'Everyone hated her. I don't think she had a friend in the world besides me, and I deserted her, too.'

'What about her husband?'

'He died. She was eighteen when she married him—Henrietta Stuart, one of the most exciting debutantes of her season, incredibly beautiful. He was in the import-export business, had offices all over the world, Africa, India, New

York, Hong Kong. He died two years after the marriage, and Henrietta was a widow at twenty —a very merry widow, notorious, in fact, if some of the tales are to be believed.'

'Wealthy?'

'Fabulously. She eventually sold the business and invested her money. It was all handled by her brokers, but I know it must have been a gigantic sum. She had a fantastic collection of jewels. She carried paste copies around with her, gorgeous things. The real ones were kept locked up in a vault in the bank.'

'What happened to them?'

'If I know Gordon Stuart, he's sold them by now—'

'What kind of person was she, Em?'

'Vain, and frivolous, and old and sharp-tongued and vile tempered. She was confined to a wheelchair a lot of the time, but she could get around with a cane when she really wanted to. She had flaming red hair, outrageously dyed, and blazing blue eyes and pathetically withered skin like yellowing paper. She demanded constant attention—and got it. Whenever she thought I was growing interested in some man we'd run across, she'd pretend to get sick and make me stay at her bedside and read to her—I've read all of Dickens and Thackeray and George Eliot three or four times over! When she was in top form, she could be coy and flirtatious with all the old gentlemen at the hotels we stopped at. She was once a great beauty, and she never got over it. She was—pathetic, really. I felt sorry for her. She used to drive me to desperation, but when I threatened to leave she'd look so desolate and alone that I just couldn't bring myself to actually leave.'

'Was she stingy?'

'Not with me. I always had new clothes, new books, records, anything I wanted besides the attention of others. She gave me a pearl necklace, one time, real pearls—I have them in a safe deposit box. She had been really close to my mother, and she often said I was like her own daughter. The old monster was affectionate in her way. She was just so spoiled and autocratic and had to have someone to boss around. I suppose it wasn't so bad. I travelled all over Europe. I wore expensive clothes. I went to all the operas and concerts and museums. But one day I looked at myself in the mirror and realized that I was twenty-two years old and had never had a love affair in my life and—it scared me. I knew that as long as I stayed with Henrietta I would never have a normal life. That worried me—'

Billie shook her head, unable to visualize a

life without men flocking around her.

'You mean you've *never* been in love?' she asked, incredulous.

'No—' I replied, hesitantly.

Billie did not come right out and call me a liar, but she smiled in a particularly knowing way and shook her head slowly. She picked up a mascara pencil and began to draw careful black lines about her eyes. 'You must tell me about Gordon Stuart,' she said lightly.

'What makes you ask about him?'

'Dearest, no woman harbours as much hatred for a man as you harbour for Gordon Stuart unless—'

'Unless what?'

'Unless there's *been* something,' she said calmly.

'He's thirty-nine years old,' I protested.

'And you're twenty-five. So?'

'He's smooth and polished and—I suppose you'd think him handsome. He never did a day's work in his life, although he piddles with stocks and investments and always managed to run through all the money Henrietta let him get hold of. He never came around much, but when he did it was always because he wanted something.'

'And?'

'And several years ago he lost everything in

some bogus investment and needed money desperately. Henrietta wouldn't give it to him. He thought he could get to her through me, and—he was very charming and persuasive and I was nineteen years old and very impressionable. He told Henrietta that he wanted to marry me, and I believed him. So did she. She gave him several thousand pounds and told him to leave us both alone. He did. I didn't see him again for three years, and by that time I was able to see him without any illusions.'

'He sounds fascinating,' Billie remarked. She put the pencil down and picked up a small jar of violet eye-shadow. She began to rub it smoothly on her lids. 'Do you think he'll come to see us in Brighton?'

'I certainly hope not.'

'I wonder why he wants the house so much? She left everything else to him. Curious, don't you think?'

'I don't know why he wants it, but I do know he's not going to get it. I've waited a long time for an opportunity like this—'

'Hell hath no fury,' Billie remarked, getting up from the dresser and tossing her tawny gold hair. 'Let's go to the kitchen and make some sandwiches. I told a couple of people we were leaving in the morning, and they might stop by for a few minutes tonight.'

'I wondered why you were putting on all the paint. A couple, you say?'

'Just Dirk and Terry, and perhaps Philip and Doug and the Todd twins. Steve, if he can get off work, and—'

'We'd better make a *lot* of sandwiches,' I said wryly.

Twenty minutes later we were waiting in the living room. A plate of sandwiches set on the coffee table, a tray of canapes beside it. Billie's admirers would furnish the liquor—in great quantities, usually, although neither Billie nor I drank much at all. Although it was almost eleven, she looked as alert and vivacious as a school girl waiting for her first party. She wore a dark gold dress with a skirt several inches above her knees, and her hair was pulled back in a pony tail and fastened with a black ribbon. The mod, mad fashions were ideal for Billie and she wore them with flair. I was more conservative.

'Em—' she said.

'Yes?'

'I wonder if Burt Reed really *did* murder Henrietta Stern?'

'Of course he did. The police found the axe buried under some shrubbery behind his cottage. It still had bloodstains and his fingerprints were all over it.'

'But he claimed he was innocent, to the very last—'

'What would you have done under the circumstances?'

She shivered. 'Just the same, he died in his cell at the jail before they could bring him to trial and convict him. I wonder—'

'What?'

'It gives me the shivers. The mere thought of it—'

'You don't have to go with me, Billie. I'm perfectly capable of going alone.'

'I wouldn't dream of missing it,' she said firmly.

Billie considered herself an authority on the Stern case. As soon as she had discovered my connection with the crime, she had rushed straight to the library and looked up all the newspaper accounts of the murder. She had read them all over and over and had been eager to discuss them with me, although at first she was afraid to mention it. I told her quite calmly that I didn't mind discussing the crime, and that was all the encouragement she needed.

All the newspapers called it one of the bloodiest crimes in years, and they had spared the public none of the gory details. For a week it had been the sensation of the tabloids, and then Burt Reed had died in his cell and other stories began to ease it from prominence.

Burt Reed owned a small cottage on the boundary of Henrietta's Brighton estate. According to the newspaper accounts, he was a crusty old fisherman who had always lived off the sea. He had made enough money to send his son to medical school, and he had been building an addition on his cottage at the time of the crime. There had been a dispute about the boundary line. Henrietta claimed he was building on her property, and he told her to go hang. She called in a surveyor and proved that part of the addition did in fact extend over the line, and Reed had had to stop building. He had been extremely vindictive about it, cursing her in public and once, according to reports, threatened to kill the old witch. On the night of November ninth Henrietta's body was found on the front porch of her house. Her head had been severed, one arm cut off and the trunk horribly mutilated. The police arrested Reed immediately, even before they found the axe. Two days after his arrest he had a heart attack in his cell. The newpaper reporters said it was a just death, although they felt slightly cheated since there would be no sensational trial, no conviction.

'I've never slept in a house where a murder was committed,' Billie remarked. 'I hope

I *can* sleep.'

'It's all over and done with,' I said firmly.

'I wonder—'

'You read too many detective stories, Billie!'

'The son—what was his name? Oh yes, George, George Reed. He claims his father is innocent. He dropped out of medical school, you know, said he would prove his father's innocence if it was the last thing he did. The newspapers made quite a thing out of it—such a belligerent young man, according to all I read. There was a picture of him in one of the tabloids. He's very good looking in a sullen sort of way. I wonder if you knew him?'

'I doubt it.'

'But you could have met him,' she insisted.

'I suppose it's possible, Billie.'

'It still amazes me that the newspapers didn't get onto your trail. I would have thought they'd have found out and exploited you like they did everyone else connected with the case.'

'I can thank Dr Clarkson for that, and Officer Stevens of the Brighton police. If I remember anything, I'll make a full report. I agreed to that, and they agreed to keep my name out of the papers.'

'Just think,' Billie said, 'if you hadn't left when you did—it's too terrible to think about!'

'If I hadn't left,' I replied calmly, 'Henrietta would probably still be alive. I—I'm going to have to learn to forgive myself for that. She was a wretched old woman—vile, vindictive, a terror, but she was kind to me at times. I deserted her—and she left me the house. It's—it's hard to know that you're partly responsible for someone's death.'

'Em, you can't blame yourself,' Billie protested gently.

'I do, though. Dr Clarkson believes that's partly the cause of my amnesia. The shock of seeing it happen was terrible, of course, and the thought that it might never have happened if I'd been there caused me to black it out of my mind. The shock and the guilt feelings were too much to bear.'

'If you'd stayed, you might have been murdered yourself.'

'Yes, I suppose that's true.'

'It amazes me that you can be so calm about it.'

'I—it's not easy,' I replied.

I got up from the sofa and walked over to the window. I pulled back the dusty green curtain and looked out at the foggy night. I could see the coloured lights from the dance hall glowing through the mist, and even from this distance I could hear the sound of music, muffled, dim. Billie sensed my apprehension. She came to stand beside me.

'I'm sorry,' she said quietly. 'I feel like such a fool—'

'Don't,' I whispered.

I took her hand and forced myself to smile, but the smile trembled on my lips. 'Don't,' I repeated. 'I owe you so much—you and Clive and Dr Clarkson. You've helped me to a new life, bright and exciting and full of noise, full of promise. It's—so wonderful, after so many years of being dependent on someone else. I've got to protect that new life, and the only way I can protect it is to stop running away, mentally as well as physically. Going back there is going to be hard, and yes, I'm afraid, but I know it's something I've got to do.'

'Of course,' Billie said, her voice very quiet. Her enormous brown eyes were sad and full of understanding, and I smiled again, a much brighter smile.

'Let's keep it light—' I said, moving away from the window and going to put a record on the phonograph. 'We'll go to Brighton and look over the house and decide whether or not I want to sell it—but not to Gordon, of course—and we'll swim and relax and you can finish your Dostoyevsky, and in a few days we'll come back, both tanned, both ready to set

London on its ear!'

Billie grinned, glad that the awkward moment was over.

'That's the spirit!' she exclaimed. 'I do think you should buy a bikini, though, Em. It's a shame, with your figure, too....'

The phonograph started playing, much too loudly, and the doorbell rang and a man who looked like Jean Paul Belmondo came in with a set of bongo drums. He sat down in a corner and began to beat them in time to the music, and the doorbell rang again and the Todd twins came bursting in, both waving bottles of wine, both fierce looking with burning black eyes and shaggy black hair. In thirty minutes the room was jammed with people, people who shouted and laughed and filled the air with smoke and boisterous revelry. I smiled and nodded and pretended I was enjoying myself while Billie cavorted and danced. More people came, and some fashion designer was swirling bolts of violently coloured material across the room, and someone else was draping them over all the furniture, and everyone laughed, everyone smiled, and all the while I was dreading the morning and the trip I knew I must take into my so recent past.

CHAPTER THREE

The air was strongly laced with a salty tang, and the waves washed over the grey shingles with a monotonous rhythm, leaving behind a residue of seaweed and foam. We had passed the town and were driving down a treacherous dirt road that would lead to the Stern place. It was an isolated spot, and the road wound through heavily wooded areas. We could catch occasional glimpses of the sea through open spaces, but there was no sign of a house, no sign that anyone lived in this bleak, desolate stretch.

'I thought it would at least be *civilized*,' Billie remarked testily. 'When one says Brighton one visualizes a glamorous resort town crowded with tourists and expensive little shops. *This* isn't Brighton.'

The car shot over a particularly nasty jolt in the road, and I gripped the steering wheel tightly. Clive had loaned us his car for the trip and I didn't want to return it to him with a broken spring.

'I think you're hopelessly lost, Em, to be perfectly honest about it. I've got such a headache, and here we are in the middle of nowhere—'

The road smoothed out, and we passed clumps of more formal trees, interspersed with shrubbery. Suddenly the trees were behind us and we were on a broad road that ran directly beside the sea. The sunlight was dazzling on the water, making silvery patterns on the grey, and the sky beyond was a soft green, misty on the horizon. Even Billie was silenced by the beauty of it. We passed an ancient cottage with the skeleton frame of an addition half built on one side, the yellow boards already beginning to weather. I saw an old boat overturned in the sand on the other side of the house, and ragged fishing nets stretched on poles near the water.

A large red dog darted out from under the front steps of the cottage and barked at the car as we passed. A man stepped out to silence the dog, but there wasn't time for me to get a good look at him. Billie said it must have been George Reed. She peered eagerly through the rear window, but he had already gone inside. She was extremely excited now, all her petulant disappointment gone. The road suddenly made a large curve, winding down to the sea. We passed through a heavily wooded area and, suddenly, the road ended, abruptly, and we were in front of the Stern house.

We got out of the car, and neither of us said a word for a moment. We had seen photographs of the place, of course, but they had not prepared us for anything like this.

'I refuse to believe it,' Billie said.

'It's—not too cheerful, is it?' I remarked.

'The perfect place for a murder,' she whispered.

The Stern place had been built at the turn of the century, and it must once have been both elegant and impressive with its turrets and gables and its large veranda, but now it was bleak and foreboding, a monstrosity of a place, the grey boards weather beaten and crusted with salt, the windows murky and dark, the blue shutters hanging loosely. It was two stories, and there were wings sprawling out on either side. A shaggy green lawn led down to a desolate beach, tall weeds growing among the white sand, and there was a large old boathouse at the water's edge, its roof half collapsed, and a wooden pier that looked extremely dangerous. Woods grew thickly on three sides of the house, tall black trees with limbs tortured by the sea winds and twisted into grotesque shapes.

I had a curious feeling as I stood there looking up at the house. Although the sun was shining brightly and the day was warm, I felt a chill. I seemed to hear barely audible whispers that warned me to turn back, and the dark recesses of the front veranda seemed to throng with invisible figures. There, right on the front porch, not ten feet away, a woman had been horribly murdered, and the whole house seemed to be permeated with a kind of evil that hung over it like a pall, dark, sinister. I considered myself a highly sensible person, not at all given to fancy, but I could not shake this sensation, no matter how hard I tried.

'Well—' Billie said, her hands on her hips.
'Do you—feel something, too?' I asked.
'Scared,' she retorted.
'But—it's so ridiculous. I feel it, too.'
'What shall we do?'
'We could drive back to Brighton,' I suggested. 'I—I'll find a real estate agent and turn the house over to him to sell. We don't *have* to stay here, you know.'
'We're grown women,' she said firmly.
'I know.'
'Not little children afraid of spooks.'
'You're right.'
'It's just a house, Emmalynn.'
'Of course it is. Just a—house.'

'We have to be brave,' she replied flippantly. 'Can you imagine how they would laugh back in London if we told them we were frightened so easily? I mean, the place probably has real charm—somewhere. It's been deserted for six months. Any house would look dreary under those circumstances.'

Billie walked boldly up the front steps and stood on the porch, turning around to encourage me to follow. She wore a short shift of black and white squares, and her hair was completely hidden by a bright red turban, her eyes concealed by dark glasses. She lounged against the bannister, and it was exactly like one of those arty magazine layouts where wildly dressed models posed against incongruous backgrounds. I smiled at the thought, and some of my apprehension vanished.

'We might as well make the most of it,' Billie said. She began to look for bloodstains while I fumbled in my purse for the key to the front door. I had just taken it out when we heard footsteps approaching. Billie seized my arm, and for a moment both of us were panic stricken.

A man walked around the corner of the house, coming from somewhere in the back, and he strolled casually up to the steps and stood looking at us. He didn't seem to be at all surprised or alarmed. He smiled. It was a dazzling smile, and the man was dazzlingly handsome by any standards. He wore a sleeveless sweat shirt and a pair of blue jeans with the pants cut off at the knees, the edges ragged. He was of medium height and powerfully built, with strong, muscular arms and immense shoulders, and his skin was bronzed by the sun. His hair was shaggy, curling about his neck and ears and falling in thick waves over his forehead, light brown and streaked with sun-bleached blond strands. His eyes were a very light blue, contrasting vividly with the dark complexion.

'Emmalynn?' he said.

I stared at him without recognition.

'I am Emmalynn Rogers,' I said.

He looked at me for a moment, the smile still curling on his wide sensual mouth. He jammed his hands in the pockets of his jeans and tilted his head to one side.

'You don't know me?' he asked.

'Do I?'

He grinned. 'Then it's true,' he said. 'Dr Clarkson wrote telling me to expect you, although he didn't say what time of day. He told me about your—uh—amnesia. You *really* don't know me?'

'I'm sorry,' I replied.

'Boyd,' he said, 'Boyd Devlon. I worked for Mrs Stern, taking care of the place, running errands, driving the Rolls when she wanted to go to town for something. I lived in the carriage house, and after the—after she died, the lawyers arranged for me to stay on as caretaker until such a time as the house was disposed of. Now that it's yours, of course, I'm no longer officially employed, but I thought I'd better stay on a few days to see if you needed anything.'

'Why—that was very thoughtful of you, Mr Devlon.'

'It used to be Boyd,' he said, his blue eyes full of amusement.

'Did it?'

'Indeed it did,' he replied.

His voice was deep and husky, a warm, intimate voice. Boyd Devlon was one of those men who radiate an instant and instantly fascinating charm. He was rugged and virile and completely at ease with himself and the world. In his ragged clothes, with his shaggy hair he could have stepped into a drawing room and been as confident as he was as he stood at the bottom of the steps now. I wondered why Henrietta would have allowed such a man to work for her. She had clung to me possessively, and she had always been on guard against men who might attract me away from her. It would seem that a man like Boyd Devlon would have been the last person she would have wanted anywhere near me.

Billie tugged at my arm impatiently.

'Oh,' I said, 'forgive me. May I introduce my friend Miss Mead, Mr Devlon.'

'Hello there,' Boyd Devlon said.

'Enchanted,' Billie replied. 'Absolutely.'

Boyd Devlon grinned boyishly, pleased at her obvious admiration. Something about his manner suggested that he was accustomed to being admired by women and might even take it for granted. I supposed it was all part of his charm. Billie took off her sunglasses and toyed with them. A whole herd of wild horses couldn't have turned her away from the house now.

'How long do you intend to stay, Miss Rogers?' he asked, and I noticed that he used the more formal address this time.

'Two or three days—perhaps a week. I want to inspect the house, get to know it. I'll probably decide to sell it, but I want to look it over before I make any definite decision.'

'It's an intriguing old place,' he remarked.

'Are all the rooms open?' I asked.

'All the downstairs, and the bedrooms upstairs. Both wings are shut, the doors locked, the furniture covered in sheets—just like before.

There are over thirty rooms, as you know.'

'Are there?'

'Not counting the attics and the cellar.'

'You're living in the carriage house?'

'There's an apartment over it. I'm staying there.'

'I'd like very much for you to stay, Mr Devlon. It's rather—isolated here and—there'll probably be a lot of things you can do for us. If you wish, you can consider yourself on salary again until we leave.'

'Fine,' he replied, nodding. 'I'll start by bringing your suitcases inside.'

I unlocked the front door and Billie and I stepped into a vast hallway with a staircase at the other end that curled up to the second floor. There was barely enough light coming through the opened door to reveal atrocious blue and violet wallpaper and ponderous black oak furniture arranged along the wall. The carpet was dark burgundy and a dusty chandelier hung from the ceiling, veiled with cobwebs. A strong odour of mildew and decay filled the air, a sour smell that was extremely unpleasant.

Boyd Devlon came in with the suitcases and set them down by the door. He stood with his hands resting lightly on his thighs.

'I'm afraid there's no electricity,' he informed us. 'They cut it off months ago—telephone too, I'm afraid. You can have them turned back on, of course, but it'll take a few days. In the meantime, you'll have to use candles and oil lamps. There are plenty of both around.'

'No electricity?' I said.

'I've always adored candlelight,' Billie remarked.

'There's an old gas stove in the kitchen, and a butane tank, so cooking will be no problem.'

We stood in the hall for a moment, all three silent. The house seemed to surround us, engulf us. It seemed to have a life of its own, and I tried once again to shake the curious sensation of dread. Boyd Devlon was silhouetted against the doorway, strong, male, a comforting presence at the moment. A ray of sunlight slanted through the door and touched his head. His sun-bleached brown hair glistened, and his bronzed skin seemed to gleam. I was very glad Billie and I were not going to be completely alone here. The house was sinister enough in mid-afternoon, and I could imagine how it must seem when darkness fell.

'Would you like me to go for groceries?' he inquired. 'You'll need supplies if you intend to stay for a few days.'

'Yes,' I replied. 'I could make a list, I suppose—or, better yet, you just get whatever you think we'll need for tonight and breakfast in the morning, and I'll go myself tomorrow and get anything else.'

I gave him my car keys and took out some money, but he refused to take the money, saying he would charge the groceries from Widow Murphy who had a grocery store down the beach that all the people in this area patronized. I asked him about running water and was relieved to find that the house still had it. He told us how to find the bedrooms and then left, strolling across the porch and down the steps. We heard him start the car and drive off. We exchanged looks there in the dimly lighted hall.

'Well?' I said.

'No man should be that good looking,' Billie replied. 'It's criminal. He knows you, Em. Did you see how friendly he was at first, like there'd been something between you?'

'You imagined it,' I said.

She shook her head. 'No, I didn't. That smile—and he said you used to call him Boyd. Oh, Em—how maddening to think you might have had a love affair you can't *remember*—'

'It's highly unlikely,' I replied. 'Henrietta would never have permitted it, and—I'm not much for love affairs, particularly with men who look like Boyd Devlon.'

'You said you must have quarrelled with her

about something out of the ordinary—something violent enough to make you leave her. Can't you see—you'd been having a love affair with Boyd Devlon and she found out about it and threatened to fire him, and you said it was your life and you'd never give him up, and—'

'You also see too many cheap movies,' I replied firmly.

'It *could* have happened,' Billie insisted.

'Not to me, and I know I could never be seriously attracted to a man like Boyd Devlon—he's too good-looking, too confident. There's something about him—'

'Magnetism,' she said.

'No, something else. I—I can't quite place it. Don't you think it odd that a man like him would be content to work for a cantankerous old woman and then be caretaker of a crumbling old seaside estate? Caretakers are usually decrepit old men who can't do anything else. Boyd Devlon could do anything he wanted. Certainly he could do better than this—'

'Maybe he has a past—' she suggested.

'Oh, Billie—'

'Or maybe the life suits him,' Billie protested. 'Some men don't want to waste their lives chasing after money and status. Other things are more important to them. He's the outdoor type—that glorious tan, like a bronze

Apollo! Maybe he simply wants to be free. I can't visualize him juggling stocks and bonds or scraping and bowing in diplomatic circles. He's an individual—does as he pleases, dresses as he pleases, thumbs his nose at the rest of the world. I think it's terribly romantic.'

'You would think that.'

'Seriously, Em, you did know him. I can't help but wonder how *well*—'

'I suppose we'll find out sooner or later.'

'Yes—' She looked around at the vast hall, examining the wallpaper and inspecting the ornately carved black oak furniture. 'You don't remember any of this?' she asked.

I shook my head.

'I can't get over it. You lived here for almost half a year, and you didn't even know where the bedrooms were. He had to tell you. This place is weird, Em. It's creepy. Just think, right out there on the porch—' She cut herself off abruptly, and we stared at each other.

'I wish I could pretend it was just a fun adventure,' Billie said, her voice serious. 'I tried at first, but—'

'I know,' I said.

'What are we going to do?'

'I suggest we go select our bedrooms,' I said. 'There'll be plenty of time to change before he returns, and I for one would like a hot shower.

We can cook dinner when he gets back with the groceries, and later on we can make plans—'

We walked down the hall and up the spiral staircase that curled darkly to the second floor. Dust was everywhere, and the air was fetid. We would have to do quite a lot of cleaning if we intended to stay here for a few days, I thought. The house had been closed up tight, and decay had already begun to encroach, working slowly and steadily. I was determined to throw open all the windows and bring light and air back into the house, at least into the rooms we would be using.

The upper hallway was long and wide. The curtains were drawn back from the windows at both ends, and sunlight poured through, long rays stirring with dust motes. The staircase continued to curl on up to the attics above. We stood in the hall. The lower half was covered with dark wormwood wainscoting, dark brown and orange wallpaper reaching on up to the brown ceiling. At either end the hall turned to extend through the wings that reached out behind the house. Fifty years ago whole families must have congregated here for the summer, and the rooms must have rung with the voices of dozens of children on holiday, but now there was only a dense silence that seemed to wrap itself around us and warn us to move quietly. There were at least a dozen doors opening off this main hallway, and all of them were closed. For some reason both Billie and I were hesitant to open any of them.

'Well, we can't just stand here—' I said finally.

'I've never seen such ugly wallpaper,' Billie replied. Both of us were speaking in whispers.

'William Morris,' I informed her. 'It was all the rage half a hundred years ago.'

'What a bizarre pattern, little birds and unicorns and strange flowers I've never seen before, maroon and orange and brown. Can you imagine *living* with such paper? And that wormwood—'

'Come on,' I whispered. 'Let's select our rooms.'

The rooms were all dark, all smelling of dust, all filled with dark heavy furniture, but we finally found two that would do. They were near the end of the hall, two bedrooms with a large dressing room and bath connecting them. I was dubious about the bathroom at first. The tub was dark green marble with black veins and all the fixtures were of tarnished brass, shaped like dolphins and lions' claws. I turned a faucet and rusty water spewed into the marble sink. After a moment the dirty yellow colour vanished and the water looked fairly clean. While I was doing this Billie discovered a huge linen closet filled with sheets and pillow cases kept fresh in heavy plastic bags, still smelling of lavender. At least we would have running water and fresh linen, I thought, slightly encouraged.

'It's not going to be so bad,' Billie remarked. 'I've always wanted to stay in a red room, and this one is certainly red—'

She stood in the opened doorway and peered into the room. Dark crimson paper covered the walls, embossed with darker red leaves, and the black oak bed had canopy and hangings of scarlet satin. Billie parted all the crimson draperies and opened the windows to let in fresh air. The canopy billowed, and the sparkling sunlight gleamed on the dark furniture. A murky blue mirror with an ornate gold frame reflected the room, and there was a chair of worn red velvet with gold fringe, a dresser with a marble top, and bouquet of brown and green wax flowers under glass setting on the enormous highboy. A framed brown lithograph of Queen Victoria hung on one wall, staring down rather accusingly at Billie as she cavorted down the room and examined all.

'It's priceless!' she exclaimed. 'It'll be rather like sleeping in a museum, but fun. This place really isn't so bad, Em. We'll just have to get used to it.'

I was glad to see some of her lively spirits return and wished that I could feel some of her sudden enthusiasm. We went down to get the suitcases and then put fresh linens on the beds. Billie went into the bathroom, hoping to master the ancient plumbing and manage a bath, and I waited in the room I had chosen for myself.

It was a little less spectacular than Billie's, the walls covered with gold and ivory striped paper, sadly faded, the carpet dark beige and the furniture golden oak with a highly vanished gloss. Yellow satin hangings draped the bed, and there was a chaise longue covered with ivory velvet. A set of prints hung on the wall depicting a Victorian family playing croquet and having a picnic by the sea. I had thrown back the heavy ivory curtains and opened all the windows. Fresh air and sunlight swirled into the room dispelling some of the dank odour and gloom.

I heard a loud shriek, then a torrent of water, and I assumed Billie had finally been successful with the bath. I stepped over to a window and leaned on the sill, looking out past the shaggy green lawn that sloped down to the beach. Water slapped against the boathouse and pier, and it sloshed over the shingles and sand. The house would never be free of the sound of the sea. From this distance it sounded like loud breathing, and the sound was not pleasant.

I watched a seagull swirl against the jade green sky, dipping down to glide over the blue-grey waves. The beach looked so desolate and bleak. It was overgrown with weeds, littered with driftwood and shells. There was a kind of beauty there, but it was a beauty that invited solemn thoughts and threatened one's sanity. The house, the beach, the atmosphere of the whole place seemed to warn, to threaten.

I heard a car approaching. In a moment Boyd Devlon drove up in front of the house and got out of the car, carrying a large sack of groceries. I stepped back a little, afraid he might look up and see me watching him. He balanced the sack in his arm and strolled across the yard. As he came nearer the house I could see the smile on his lips, a curious smile, brash, almost mischievous, and I wondered about this man who moved about so confidently, who insinuated that I had known him far better than it would have been wise to know a man like Boyd Devlon.

CHAPTER FOUR

Billie had insisted on cooking dinner herself. That was something she never did, but it was necessary for Boyd Devlon to give her lengthy instructions on how to use the stove, and I assumed the opportunity to be alone with him had more to do with it than any desire to please me. They were both in the kitchen now, and I stood on the front veranda, watching the last rays of sunlight stain the sky with dark orange banners.

It had happened out here, just a few yards from where I was standing. Billie had assured me that the bloodstains were still visible, but I did not have the courage to look for myself. I braced myself, trying not to let fear and hysteria grip me. I had not wanted to come, but now I was here and I had to be sensible about it. I couldn't let my fancy run away with me. A horrible, grisly murder had been committed, but it had happened six months ago, and the house was just a house. It was not haunted. It was not under a curse. It was just old and decrepit. The veranda was just a veranda, even if an old woman had been horribly mutilated with an axe and all the bloodstains hadn't been scrubbed away.

Why had it happened out here? I wondered. What was she doing on the veranda? She had been all alone in the old house. According to the papers Boyd Devlon had been in Brighton visiting friends the night it happened. He had discovered the body when he returned to the house in the early hours of the morning. For a moment, as I stood gripping the railing and staring at the beach without seeing it, I gave my imagination free reign. She may have been sitting in the parlour, very late, and someone knocked on the door. She had hobbled down the hall with her cane, and she had peered out the window at whoever stood standing there in the shadows. She had opened the door and stepped out on the veranda, ready to argue, and then the axe began to hack and cut and she had fallen, screaming, and the blood gushed and flooded the porch and ran between the boards and dripped down the steps. The head had rolled across the porch and lodged against the pickets of the very railing I gripped so tensely now.

I closed my eyes, and my heart was pounding. No, I told myself, no! I can't think about it. It's over. They arrested Burt Reed. They found the axe buried beneath the shrubbery in back of his cottage. He died in jail. His son claims the man was innocent, but the police arrested him just the same. It's over. It's over—and I must not think about it. I can't let myself think about it—

I wanted to run back into the house and tell Billie to pack her things and I wanted to get in the car and drive away from this place and forget it ever existed, but I couldn't. I couldn't run away again. I took a deep breath and folded my arms around my body. There was a gentle breeze, and it cooled my cheeks and blew locks of auburn hair about my temples. The moment of panic departed, and I was calm again.

I thought about Henrietta Stern as I had known her. All her glory was vanished by that time, and she was just a miserable old woman who drifted about Europe with a paid companion, but I knew that years ago, decades ago, she had been the toast of society, a flamboyant, eccentric beauty who had sparkled like a Roman candle for a few brief years. She had made many enemies, and she had bragged about them. Even during the years I had known her and travelled with her feuds had kept her in a constant state of excitement. A month never passed that there was not a running battle with someone. Henrietta loved a scrap, and the only thing that bothered her was that her opponents were no longer worthy. She fought with porters and clerks and landlords when once, she assured me, she had fought with statesmen and powerful matrons, the men who shaped history and the women who changed it. She was a pitiful creature, who mourned the glories of the past while despising the bleakness of the present.

People had tolerated her because of her wealth. Money, or the promise of money, had smoothed the way wherever she went, and the most outrageous conduct was overlooked because Henrietta Stern was known to have a fortune, although most of it was tied up in real estate and investments. A few people remembered her—one of those names that had blazed in the headlines of all the papers during the late twenties and early thirties before vanishing into oblivion. It was ironic that after almost thirty years of obscurity she should have hit the headlines again, not as a celebrity of the past but as the victim of a sensational murder. The newspapers had dwelled upon the crime in great detail, but not one of them had mentioned her past glories. She had been an eccentric old woman who had chosen to stay in a crumbling seaside estate when she could have been living in a plush London apartment, and none of the reporters had been remotely interested in what she might have been thirty years before.

What a strange life she had led, and what a horrible way it had ended. I blamed myself in part for that. I couldn't help but feel that if I hadn't left her alone she would still be alive today. I had had little affection for her, but I had been grateful to her. She had rescued me when I was all alone and penniless. She had taken me all over Europe, bought me expensive new clothes, new books. She had given me a genuine pearl necklace. She had been a tyrant, demanding absolute devotion and loyalty, but, in her way, she had been fond of me. I was all she had, and I had shown my gratitude by deserting her, leaving her to be murdered in such a brutal manner.

It was not good to think about it. If I thought about it much I would have to leave quickly, while I still had my sanity.

The sky was growing darker, and I wondered how long it would take Billie to cook dinner. I privately doubted if she could even open a can without performing a surprise appendectomy, but she had been so determined that I had seen no point in arguing. I smiled, imagining her trying to cope with the ancient stove, and I half expected to hear a loud explosion at any moment. But Boyd Devlon was with her, and if I knew Billie she would make him her captive before much time had elapsed—or try. I doubted if anyone could completely subjugate a man like him.

I looked up, startled out of my revery. A car was coming down the road towards the house, the motor purring silkily. It circled the drive in front of the house and came to a stop, a sleek grey car with gleaming chrome and a black leather interior. A man got out, and at first I did not recognize him. It had been a long, long time. He came towards the veranda, and when he saw me standing there he stopped, looking up at me. A smile curled on his wide, thin lips.

Gordon Stuart had not changed. He was tall and thin with a lean, handsome face and a strong jaw, a slightly crooked nose and piercing blue eyes with lids that drooped a bit at the corners. His brows were heavy, arched demonically, and his steel grey hair was cut close to the skull. He had a ruthless face that fascinated women and disturbed men who had to do business with him. He was smooth and polished, his raw silk suit expensively tailored, his tie a dark, subdued red. But for all his surface gloss there was something of the buccaneer about Gordon Stuart. At nineteen I had been highly susceptible to his rakish charm. At twenty-five it left me unmoved. With his dubious business deals, his careless disregard for others, Gordon was a hawk in a predatory world, and I wanted to have nothing to do with him. I stared at him coldly.

'Is it really you?' he said. His voice was rough and grating, but it had a curious musical quality nevertheless. It was an attractive voice. I used to think it was like silk being torn slowly into shreds.

'Hello, Gordon,' I said.

He strolled up the steps and stood a few feet away from me, the smile still twisting on his lips. His blue eyes glittered with male appreciation, and I was glad I had changed into my new yellow dress and had brushed my long auburn locks. I felt a slight blush colouring my cheeks, and I looked away from him, remembering what I had felt for him so long ago and wondering how I could have been so naive, even at nineteen.

'You've changed,' he said.

'Have I?'

'The shy little girl with the downcast eyes and trembling mouth has blossomed into a woman—' He paused, his eyes sweeping over me. 'Quite a beautiful woman,' he added.

'What do you want, Gordon?'

'My Dear, are you afraid of me?'

'Why do you ask that?'

'You're so—defensive. I didn't come here to murder you—'

I turned and glared at him, and he chuckled quietly. 'Sorry. A mistaken choice of words. Tactless of me. This is where it happened, isn't it? Right here on this porch—'

He turned to examine the veranda as though he were examining a picture in a museum. He stepped over in front of the door and peered down at the dark stains that still streaked the boards. He shook his head slowly, one heavy black brow tilted up. There was something cold and merciless about the way he examined the place where his sister had been murdered. I knew he had never cared for her, but I wondered how anyone could be so brutally objective about anything so horrible.

'Why did you come here, Gordon?'

'Why—to see you, My Dear.'

'I find that hard to believe.'

'Do you?'

'There was a time when you weren't so eager to see me—'

He smiled the silken smile. He slid one long hand into the pocket of his jacket and toyed with his tie with the other. 'So you still hold that early indiscretion against me?' he said smoothly. 'Good. That means it isn't quite over. You still think about me. Women may hate me for a while but they never forget me.'

'You're incredibly arrogant, Gordon.'

'Perhaps, but I'm no hypocrite. Honesty is so often mistaken for arrogance these days. People want sugar coating, false modesty, sham. I've got no time for those particular virtues. I believe a man should—'

'I'm not interested in your philosophy,' I said, interrupting him.

'No? There are far more interesting subjects we can pursue. I understand you're a photographer's assistant now. Clive Courtney, no less. You started at the top. He's very in at the moment. Do you enjoy the work?'

'It's satisfactory.'

'Much more exciting than indulging the whims of a sulky old woman, I'd imagine. You were made for excitement—I sensed it years ago, when you were still just a girl. You hid your flame far too long. I'm glad to see it glowing.'

I didn't reply. I stood by the railing, cool, distant, trying hard to control myself. He was goading me, gently, cautiously, trying to make me break down so that I would be easier to manage. Gordon Stuart brought out all my bad qualities, and it was hard to hold them in check. I wanted to shout at him and order him off the property, but I knew that was what he would like for me to do so that he could be calm and superior.

'Are you in Brighton for long?' I inquired, my voice frostily polite.

'For a few days.'

'What brings you here?'

'Oh—a number of things.'

'Why do you want the house, Gordon? We both know that's why you've come here.'

The abrupt question seemed to catch him off guard. He frowned slightly, a deep crease between his brows. Gordon Stuart liked to handle things his own way, use his own tactics, and it irritated him that I had disobeyed the rules of polite banter. He ran his fingers over his steel grey hair and gave me a little nod.

'You're still as sharp as ever,' he said.

'I know you. I know you never want anything without a reason. Why do you want the house?'

'It should have been mine, you know,' he said quietly. 'Henrietta left everything to me in the original will. The courts favoured the second will, as you know, but I'm still a bit dubious about it—' He shrugged his shoulders elegantly. 'But that squabble is over. It's just a run down old house that has no real value.'

'Then why are you so intent on having it?'

'I have my reasons, Emmalynn.'

'I'd like to hear them.'

'You wouldn't understand. Business reasons. I—uh—need a tax loss. I intend to turn this place into a resort hotel—a disastrous venture, of course, but a very smart one taxwise, my lawyers assure me. I'll pay you handsomely—very handsomely, because you're Emmalynn and because I have a fond affection for you.'

I smiled wryly. 'You're not talking to a nineteen-year-old girl now, Gordon,' I said. 'The house isn't for sale.'

'No?'

'Not to you.'

'You still hold a grudge?'

'Call it that if you like. You're not going to have it.'

'Come now. Be sensible. There's no earthly reason why you should want to keep it yourself, and I will pay you far more than you could get from anyone else.'

'You're wasting your time, Gordon.'

He stared at me, his blue eyes flat, his lips pressed tightly together. Gordon Stuart was completely without scruples, and he was accustomed to having his way. I didn't doubt he would use any tactics, fair or foul, to get what he wanted, and I could see that he intended to have the house. I stared at him calmly, not at all intimidated. For a moment he seemed about to lash out, and then he relaxed, forcibly. I could see the effort it took for him to maintain that silken poise.

'I have plenty of time,' he said quietly.

'Do you?'

'All the time in the world. I must warn you, Emmalynn, I usually get what I'm after—' The words were soft and silken, but I knew they contained a threat.

'Not this time,' I promised.

He smiled. 'I can be very persuasive—'

'I seem to remember that.'

'Ah, yes,' he replied. 'I was a fool, Emmalynn. I realize that now. I should have swept you away from her. I should have removed you from her clutches and introduced you to a world more worthy of your charms. It's not too late—'

I shook my head slowly.

'It won't work,' I said. 'Not with this girl.'

He grinned and shook his head. 'It seems I've lost my touch,' he remarked. 'Or perhaps I've merely underestimated you. Well—' He shrugged his shoulders again in that curiously elegant manner. 'We'll see what we shall see. It should prove very interesting. Tell me—is it true about your illness?'

I nodded.

'You actually saw the crime committed? And you don't remember anything about being in Brighton?'

'That's right,' I replied.

'I should think that would be—quite uncomfortable. Is it a permanent thing?' His voice was very casual, too casual.

'Dr Clarkson doesn't think so. He thinks coming back here will cause me to remember —everything.'

'And then?'

'And then I'll make a report to the police and it will all be over.'

'Highly unusual—' he said, frowning. 'Hmm,' he seemed to be lost in thought. 'It must have taken a great deal of courage for you to come back here—under the circumstances.'

'What do you mean by that?'

'Oh—nothing, really. You actually saw the murder? Reed's son says his father didn't kill her—you must know that. He's been running all over the countryside trying to find evidence, trying to find proof that someone else did it. He's even had the gall to question me. It would be rather dangerous, wouldn't it, if his father really was innocent? You saw the murder, and when you remember—'

'Are you trying to frighten me?'

'I couldn't dream of it, My Dear. Very

ungentlemanly. I wonder—' He paused again, and I could almost see a devious idea planting itself in his mind. 'This illness—very unusual. Very delicate things, all these mental disturbances. You could remember today, or tomorrow, or—why, you might even go insane.' He spoke quietly, thoughtfully, but his words caused a cold chill to grip me. 'I wonder if you're legally competent to handle an inheritance?'

'You're foul,' I whispered.

'It might be worth investigation. Yes, it just might be.'

'Dr Clarkson—'

'Dr Clarkson could be managed,' he said smoothly.

'Leave me alone, Gordon.'

'I fight very dirty, My Dear. You should know that.'

'Leave—'

'Be smart,' he said. 'Don't fight me. I—uh—wouldn't want to hurt you.'

'You don't intimidate me.'

'No? Be smart,' he repeated. 'Pack your bags and leave this place. Sell it to me. I'll pay you handsomely, and you can take a nice trip to the south of France or Majorca and have yourself a holiday.'

'Not a chance,' I said.

'Very well—'

'Goodbye, Gordon.'

'Goodbye, Emmalynn. I'll—keep in touch.'

He took my hand and pressed it warmly, and he nodded his head, mocking me with this sham gallantry. I pulled my hand away, and Gordon grinned. He gave me a lingering look with his piercing blue eyes, and then he left. He walked down the steps and strolled towards the car, poised, elegant, a man completely confident of victory. My hands were trembling, and I felt cold all over, but I didn't intend to give way to the violent emotions that threatened to overcome me. I stood rigidly on the veranda, watching him get into his car and drive away. I didn't hear Billie step outside. I wasn't even aware of her until she touched my arm.

'Em—are you all right?'

'Yes. I—I think so.'

'I heard. I came to tell you dinner was ready, and I heard everything he said. My God—'

'I'm not afraid of him.'

'He's incredible! Why—I was scared spitless just *listening*. Em—I think—shouldn't we leave, go back to London?'

'That's exactly what he'd like for us to do!'

'But—'

I shook my head violently. 'I'm not going

to let him scare me off that easily. He's vile—perfectly vile—but there's not a thing he can do to me. I don't intend to run!'

'I don't understand. Why does he want this house? Why could he possibly want it?'

'I don't know, Billie,' I said, 'but I intend to find out.'

CHAPTER FIVE

There were bound to be noises in an old house. Windows would rattle, boards would creak, the foundations would settle, and there would undoubtedly be rats scurrying in the walls. I was determined not to let any of them bother me. I was determined to sleep soundly and get up in the morning to a busy, active day. There was much to be done. We hadn't explored the house yet, and I wanted to go through all the closed rooms and examine them. Some of the furniture might fetch a good price on the antique market, and the house itself could be placed in the hands of a real estate agent who would eventually sell it for me—to anyone besides Gordon Stuart. I was exhausted after a long, nerve-wracking day, and I felt sure I would be able to sleep as soon as I rested my head on the pillow.

I snuffed out the candle and got into bed. The sheets were of coarse linen texture, but they were deliciously scented. It was after midnight, for Billie and I had sat up in the parlour for hours after dinner, talking. She was asleep now, perfectly cosy in her red room, but I was finding it harder to slip into unconsciousness. The windows were all open, and the breeze caused the curtains to billow into the room. In the semi-darkness, they looked remarkably like ghostly figures stirring restlessly, whispering inaudible warnings. I closed my eyes, banishing the fantasy.

The little portable travelling clock on my bedside table ticked loudly and monotonously. I hoped the monotony of the sound would lull me to sleep. I could hear the waves washing over the shore. The sound was so much like heavy breathing that it was slightly unnerving. It sounded as though someone were standing just outside the window, breathing heavily, or panting. Nonsense, I told myself, nonsense. Think about pleasant things. Think about the studio and Clive and the book. Think about the flat in Chelsea and parties and bright colours. Don't think at all. Just sink, sink slowly into darkness. Black, welcome, cool, sleep.

It didn't work. My mind wouldn't obey. I thought about the ugly black trees that surrounded the house on three sides, dark woods, full of darkness, cutting the house off, shrouding it. I thought about the desolate beach with the decrepit boathouse and the pier, rotten wood, barnacles and decay. I thought about all the rooms shut up tight, dust covers over all the furniture, cobwebs stretching across the corners, and I thought about the long, dark halls, and I could hear stealthy footsteps creeping along. The house is old, and it's settling. A scurrying sound. Rats. The curtains billowed, flapping gently, slap, slap, a sucking sound, slap again, the stiff material rustling. A window frame rattled loudly downstairs. Someone breaking in. No, a sudden gust of wind.... Black shadows, lulling, surrounding, whispering....

I saw her hobbling along the hall, her dyed red hair piled untidily on top of her head, her withered old face smiling in anticipation of a fight. She loved a fight more than anything. Brighton is so dull, no one to fight with, and then Burt Reed started building the extra room on his cottage, a wonderful excuse for a good scrap. She hobbled down the hall, her gnarled old hand gripping the head of the ebony cane.

I could hear her chuckling as she peered through the window at the side of the door, seeing a dark shadow standing in the grey, misty shadows on the porch. She opened the door, and I saw the blade of the axe gleaming in the moonlight, and I heard the horrifying noise as bones crunched, saw rivers of blood pouring over the porch and dripping down the front steps....

I sat up in bed. The house was absolutely still, frightening still. There was no noise besides the ticking of the clock. I could not even hear the sound of the sea. The curtains hung limply at the windows, not a breath of air. The tick, tick of the clock. Nothing else. I looked at the clock. The luminous dials glowed. It was almost four thirty in the morning. So I had slept, after all. I was wide awake now, tense, alert, and it didn't seem I could possibly have slept. There was no drowsiness, no feeling of groggy release. I was as awake as I had ever been in my life, every nerve stretched tight, waiting.

Waiting for what? I had been dreaming, dark wings fluttering around in my mind, puzzling pictures, shadows, Henrietta hobbling down the hall and opening the door, pain, terror, and then something had jerked away the layers of unconsciousness, ripped them aside and brought me shooting up to this state of acute awareness. My shoulders were trembling, my wrists felt limp, and my throat was dry. It had happened so suddenly that it took me a moment to realize that I was gripped with terror.

A dream. The dream awakened me. I saw it happen in my mind, and it was so bloodcurdling that I shot up in bed, wide awake, the dream gone but the horror of it still there. I tried to convince myself that it was only the dream, but I knew it wasn't. Something had awakened me with a jolt, something real, not imagined. I gripped the sheets with tight fingers. I sat paralysed, listening, but there was no noise besides the ticking of the clock. I sat for several minutes, waiting, listening, and finally some of the terror vanished and I sighed, scolding myself for my weakness. A dream, an overactive imagination, terror...I was twenty-five years old, a full grown woman, not a little girl afraid of the dark.

Misty moonlight poured through the windows suffusing the room with a foggy blue-grey light. Shadows slid along the striped wallpaper. I could see the shapes of furniture, the gigantic wardrobe, the heavy dresser, the murky mirror that reflected the moonlight. In the mirror I could see a young woman with hair spilling about her shoulders in long auburn waves, her face pale, her eyes dark, smudges of shadow under them. I lifted one hand to push back a lock of hair, and the girl in the mirror did the same.

Four thirty, almost morning. At least three more hours of sleep. No reason to be alarmed. The sun will be coming up in a little while, and all the shadows will be driven away. Sleep. It was a dream, nothing more, and it woke you up. Foolish to sit here like this, waiting, listening. Then I heard footsteps in the hall.

I caught my breath, terrified. The floorboards creaked loudly, and I was quite sure that someone was walking down the hall right outside. There could be no mistake about it. I gripped the sheet so tightly that I almost tore the coarse linen fabric. A footstep, pause, another footstep, then silence. The clock ticked, one minute passed, another, five minutes and no more footsteps. Was someone standing outside the door of my room? There was the sound of heavy breathing. Someone was standing by the door, listening, and I was sure they could hear my heart pounding. Another minute. I watched the antique brass doorknob, fascinated, certain it had turned. I had not locked the door. The doorknob turned. Did it? Ever so slightly? No. The sound of breathing was the sound of the sea, washing over the sand and lapping the shingles. A breeze stirred the curtains. They billowed as they had done earlier, fluttering white shapes dancing demonically.

Nonsense, I told myself. You're tired, upset, your nerves on edge. You had a terrible dream and it woke you up and you're imagining things. It is almost daylight. No one is standing outside the door. No one was walking stealthily down the hall.

I knew it would be impossible to sleep unless I made sure. I got out of bed and slipped a white cotton robe over my beige silk pyjamas. I opened the door to the dressing room and bath and moved slowly towards the door to Billie's room. The bathroom floor was cold to my bare feet, and there was the odour of cologne that Billie had spilled earlier in the night. If there had been a loud noise, loud enough to wake me up with a start, it would have awakened her, too.

I was almost certain there had been footsteps in the hall, not certain but almost. Perhaps it had been Billie. Perhaps she had awakened and gone downstairs to get something to eat. She was always doing that in the flat. She would eat practically nothing at dinner and then raid the icebox in the middle of the night. I shook my head, almost amused at the thought. There was nothing on God's earth that could induce Billie to go downstairs in the dark by herself in this house. She would die of starvation first. No, if there had been footsteps, they most certainly weren't Billie's. I opened the door to her room, half expecting her to be wide awake, trembling with terror.

She was curled on the bed on top of twisted sheets, wearing a pair of shortie pyjamas, a black velvet mask over her eyes. Ear plugs, too, no doubt. She was sleeping peacefully, her hair tangled on the pillow, one arm dangling over the side of the bed. Moonlight flooded the room, gilding the red walls with silver. I closed the door quietly behind me and went back to my own room.

Sleep was out of the question, at least for the present. I sat down on the edge of the bed, trying to find enough courage to do what I knew I would have to do to chase away the phantoms. There was no one in the hall, but I knew I had to make sure before I could even think of sleeping again.

It's absurd, absurd, I told myself shakily. No one would dare break into the house, not when there's a man about. Boyd Devlon is in the carriage house, and he's a light sleeper. He told us that tonight. He has a gun. He told us that, too. All the doors were locked, all the windows, and no one could have broken in without awakening him. Billie told him she was scared tonight when they were in the kitchen, and he laughed at her, told her not to worry. The carriage house is all the way in back, and he may not be such a light sleeper after all. Someone could have cut the glass on one of the French windows and reached in to unfasten the handle, like they do in mystery movies. They'd have tape to keep the glass from falling. This is absurd, absurd.

I tightened the belt of my robe and ran my hand through my hair, trying to reassure myself that there was nothing amiss. I groped on the bedside table and found the candle in its old brass holder. I found the book of matches and tried to strike one on the cover. My hands were trembling so violently that I couldn't manage anything even as simple as striking a match. I cursed, furious at myself, furious with my cowardice and my over active imagination. I used half a book of matches before I finally managed to get one properly lit. I held it over the wick of the candle, cupping my hand around the flame. The golden-orange glow flickered and began to spread in an ever widening circle.

Bathed by the misty moonlight, the room

had been subdued, quiet, but the candlelight caused violent black shadows to leap and jump on the walls. The harsh outlines of the furniture were brought into prominence, and the tears and crinkles in the old wallpaper were revealed. Whoever said candlelight was romantic? I wondered. It was ugly, wavering, dim. Better to walk in darkness than to walk with the wick of a candle flickering wildly as beads of wax spluttered in the brass holder. Nothing would have induced me to go out into the hall without it, despite the fluttering flame. I turned the doorknob that had held me fascinated a few minutes ago. I opened the door and stepped into the hall.

It was cold here. We had opened the windows at either end, hoping the fresh air would dispell some of the musty odour. I shivered, standing there in front of my door, looking up and down the length of the hall. Moonlight came in through the windows, making pools of silver at both ends, but the rest was black, thronging with shadows. A dozen people could be standing against those dark walls, watching me as I stepped timidly forward with the candle holder gripped tightly in my hand.

I walked the length of the hall, holding the candle high. The yellow glow threw shadows leaping about the William Morris wallpaper.

Curious little birds and defiant unicorns stared down at me. My back was rigid, and I moved slowly. The waves washed the shore, and the noise coming through the opened windows was suggestive. Breathing, heavy breathing. I passed the door of Billie's room. I walked on down the hall, and I almost didn't see the door that was opened. It stood ajar, hanging rather loosely on the old hinges, and I was past it before the fact that it was open registered. We had closed all the doors and locked them, hadn't we? We examined all the rooms and decided on the two we would use, and we locked the doors of those we wouldn't occupy. Hadn't we? I couldn't remember for sure.

I pushed the door back. The hinges creaked loudly. The noise was terrifying in the silence, even though I had caused it myself. The room was a great tomb of darkness, all the windows closed, the heavy draperies shut tight. There was an odour of old wax and rotting material. The flame flickered over the shredding paper that drooped on the walls, darted over the dark bulky furniture that was covered with dust. A pair of hard yellow eyes glared down at me, and I almost screamed. The eyes belonged to a stuffed eagle that perched atop the wardrobe, its wings spread wide. It looked as though it were about to swoop down and tear my face with its wicked beak. I shuddered. A terrible thing to have in a bedroom. Imagine sleeping with something like that hovering over you. I had always considered taxidermy a loathsome hobby, and the eagle only strengthened this conviction.

There was no one in the room. We had probably closed the door, and it had clicked back open. The hinges were rusty, the lock probably sprung. I was about to leave when I noticed the curious alignment of the furniture. Everything was slightly out of line, as though every piece had been pulled out and then pushed back rather carelessly. As I stood gazing, puzzled, I noticed the shredded wallpaper again, and I suddenly realized that it had been deliberately shredded. Someone had run a knife along behind it. I set the candle on a low table and bent down to examine a plum chair covered with shabby blue velvet. There was a large rip in back of the chair, and someone had reached in and dug among the stuffing. A few puffs of the stiff grey padding littered the floor. The room had been searched. Why hadn't I noticed it earlier, when we were inspecting the rooms?

I was still bending over the chair when the door slammed shut. It made an explosion of sound, and I cried out. The windows rattled. A great gust of wind battered the house. The candle flame spurted up, wavered violently for an instant and then went out. The room was pitch dark. Cold chills went up my spine, and I gripped the edge of the chair, frantic. Someone slammed the door. Someone closed me in the room. No, no, it was the wind, a gust of wind that caused the windows to rattle.

I groped in the darkness for the candle holder. I managed to find it, and I stumbled towards the door. I turned the knob. I pulled. The door did not budge. Darkness swirled around me, black, black shadows, dust, decay, and fear so real it seemed to stroke my arms and blow wisps of hair across my temples. I turned at the door frantically, on the verge of hysteria, and it flew open, slamming against the wall and almost knocking me over. It had been stuck. I sighed deeply and shook my head, ashamed of my moment of panic.

No one had slammed the door shut. No one had locked it. Absurd, absurd. No one was prowling the dark corridors. No one had broken into the house. Absurd to be out here, absurd to be imagining all sorts of things, carrying on like the heroine of an improbable suspense melodrama...back to my own bedroom, back to sleep. No more dreams, no more imagined noises. I stood in the hall, gripping the brass candle holder with its extinguished light.

Without the candlelight the hall didn't seem so black. The darkness was less impenetrable, less dense, and I could easily find my way back to my room without the aid of a candle. A candle blinded me and made the dark seem darker. I was calm now, willing to laugh at myself, willing to forget my frightened fancies.

I started back towards my room, moving resolutely, almost unaware of the darkness and the shifting shadows and the creaking floorboards. I would not say anything about this to Billie. I would go back to sleep, and in the morning, in the sunshine, this could all be put in its true perspective. I had been nervous and on edge. I had been awakened by a dream. I had given way to a too active imagination. I smiled to myself, and then I stood dead still, horrified.

There, near the top of the stairs, a dark form stood against the wall, not clear, vague, but quite real, moving along the wall towards the staircase. I closed my eyes tightly. I gripped the candle holder as though it were a log and I were drowning. I opened my eyes, sure the form would be gone, determined to be reasonable. It moved away from the wall, stood for an instant at the top of the stairs and then disappeared into the well of darkness. I dropped the candle holder. It clattered loudly. I cursed.

I darted down the hall to the staircase. I leaned over the railing and peered down into that nest of shifting shadows. There was a window over the landing, a very small window set high up, covered by a dark curtain, but a few threads of moonlight seeped through, piercing the darkness with a faint misty glow. Movement catches the eye, even when it is almost invisible movement, and I saw something moving, a shadow among shadows, creeping down the stairs.

'Who's there!' I called.

The shadow merged into shadows, and there was nothing but the echo of my voice. The house was still, silent. I peered down, angry now, all my fear submerged by the anger. The wind began to blow. The curtains at both ends of the hall billowed, flapping noisily. A floorboard creaked. Then I heard a soft sound, so soft that it was barely audible. It sounded like a chuckle, and it was the most terrifying noise I had ever heard. For a moment the sound floated up to me, and then it was gone. I could not even be sure I'd heard it.

Billie's door flew open. She charged into the hall, an oil lamp in her hand. Her hair was a tangled mass about her shoulders. Her eyes were wide. She hurried towards me, and I saw how pale she was. Her hand was trembling so vigorously that I feared she would drop the lamp over the bannister. I took it from her. In the warm yellow glow of light, the staircase was empty. The stairs circled down to the hall, and there was no one there. I set the lamp down on the post. I sighed heavily. I relaxed.

'What on earth—' Billie began.

'I had a dream.'

'A dream!'

'A—a nightmare, I guess. It woke me up.'

'Something woke me up, too. A hideous noise. It sounded like a shrill scream—'

'The wind—a door slammed. I dropped the candle holder. It clattered. Nothing is wrong. Nothing—seems to be—'

'My God, Em! How *could* you come traipsing out here alone in the middle of the night?'

'I thought I heard something. It was my imagination.'

'What was it?'

'Nothing. The wind, the house—nothing extraordinary.'

'Thank Heavens! Why when I woke up—'

'Rather early for you,' I remarked.

'It's five. I woke up and ran into your room and saw you weren't there and I almost *died*!'

'Everything's all right now,' I said.

'I thought I heard a scream, and I visualized an axe—'

She shook her head, still visibly shaken. I smiled.

'It's almost morning,' I said. 'Seems rather foolish to go back to bed now that we're both awake. Why don't we go get dressed and then make a pot of coffee. I could use a cup or two.'

'So could I. I could use something *stronger*.'

'At five in the morning?' I teased.

'I certainly could!'

We walked back to our rooms. I paused at Billie's door, my hand on her arm. 'Billie— did we lock all the doors of these rooms up here?'

'I think so. Why?'

'I just wondered. Do you remember an eagle?'

'An eagle? Have you lost your mind?'

'A stuffed eagle, perched on the top of the wardrobe in one of the rooms.'

'What a perfectly ghastly idea. No, but then we didn't go into all of the rooms. Remember? We went through all those on the other side of the hall, and then we started on this side and found these rooms and didn't go into the other four.'

'That explains it,' I said, relieved.

'Explains what? What are you talking about? Eagles—'

'I'll tell you all about it after we've had

our coffee,' I promised. 'There really isn't much to tell—'

I went into my room to dress. The first light of dawn was showing on the horizon. Daylight would come. Shadows would vanish. There had been nothing out there, no footsteps, no dark form, no soft laughter. It had all been my imagination. I tried very hard to convince myself of that.

CHAPTER SIX

A bird sang lustily, celebrating the glittering sunshine and the pure white sky. The air was invigorating, heady, blowing off the water with a salty tang. It was a breathtaking day, and I found it hard to believe that only a few short hours ago I had been prowling dark corridors and imagining terrible things. I told myself briskly that I had imagined everything, and I had half convinced myself that this was true. Just the same I was now outside, circling the house and looking for signs of forced entry. All the windows had been locked downstairs, all the doors carefully secured when I checked them from inside, but perhaps I had missed something. There might be something out here that would not have been apparent inside. I did not know exactly what I hoped to find—footprints in the ground, chipped wood on the window ledge, a board torn away. I had been unsuccessful so far. I had seen absolutely nothing that looked amiss.

It was not quite eight o'clock, and yet I felt fresh and full of energy, despite the restless night. Perhaps it was because of the glorious air and the sparkling yellow sunlight, or perhaps it was partly relief that the night was over and darkness gone. I could almost feel the blood surging in my veins, and my body felt attuned to the world, every muscle aching to be used, to feel. I wanted to rush down the slope and take off my shoes and frolic at the water's edge, and I wanted to examine the dark green leaves on the shrubbery and throw rocks at the blue jay and let the wind toss my hair in every direction. I had no idea where such vitality came from, but I was delighted with it. No depression this morning, no headache, no dark circles under my eyes. I had a feeling of release, of abandon.

Billie was still in the kitchen, drinking her sixth cup of coffee and moaning about lack of sleep but I had been unable to stay inside a moment longer. It was so glorious not to hear blaring traffic, not to smell cabbage and ale, not to see dozens of people milling around with grumpy faces as they inhaled petrol fumes and soot. London was fascinating, but there was definitely something to be said for the coast.

It would be warm later on, but there was still a slight chill in the air now. I was glad I was wearing my light knit yellow sweater and brown and yellow plaid skirt. The skirt was three inches above my knees, but I wore knee-high yellow stockings with my brown loafers. I broke a twig off a tree branch and nibbled at it, tasting sap and bark, feeling like an irresponsible child. After all, this *was* a holiday, even if it did have grim overtones. The blue jay scolded me and darted to another resting place.

A drive of crushed grey shell wound around one side of the house, bordered with beds of tiny purple flowers. I walked along it, my shoes crunching loudly on the shell. I studied all the windows I passed. They were all locked, the panes streaked with dirt but the glass unbroken. There were no footprints in the grass, still soggy with dew, no sign whatsoever of any intruder. I followed the drive to the back of the house, the ugly black tree pressing closer now, the limbs twisted. They made dark tunnels that led into deeper woods. The wind rustled the leaves, caused the branches to groan. They threw dancing shadows over this part of the drive. I stopped several yards away from the carriage house.

It was constructed of the same weathered grey wood as the house, paint peeling off the sides, the blue roof sagging slightly. The bottom floor had been converted into a garage, and the door stood open to reveal Clive's car parked beside an ancient Rolls Royce which must belong to me now. A stone staircase led up to the second floor, where Boyd Devlon stayed. I saw curtains at the windows. I wondered if it would be possible for anyone staying in the apartment to hear noises coming from the front part of the house. I doubted it. Even if Boyd Devlon *were* a light sleeper, he wouldn't hear anything if someone broke a window in the front. I stood on the drive, looking up at the curtained windows and wondering again about the man.

I did not hear him coming down the stairs. I was still staring at the windows when he called my name. I was startled. He was standing on the bottom step, watching me. I felt a slight blush colour my cheeks, and I felt guilty, as though he had caught me spying on him.

'I—I was wondering if you were up,' I said.

'Did you want something?'

'No—' I replied. 'Nothing in particular.'

'I've been up since six,' he informed me.

'I—uh—wanted to ask you about the car. The Rolls. I suppose it's mine now—or Gordon would already have taken it.'

'It's yours,' he said. 'You used to love to ride in it, remember? You sat in the back seat and said you felt like a princess in such an elegant car. You always insisted I wear my uniform when I drove you to town, although Henrietta —Mrs Stern—didn't care one way or the other. It was just a means of transportation to her.'

'It's such an old car,' I said, peering through the opened door at the dingy dove grey car with its red leather interior.

'Needs to be waxed, shined up a bit. It's still swank enough for any princess.'

'I've never had a Rolls before,' I remarked casually.

'You're very fortunate.'

'It's strange owning one now.'

Boyd Devlon didn't reply. He was looking at me in a curious way, his light blue eyes gleaming, his mouth curled in a rather melancholy smile. He wore a pair of sandals, faded brown chino pants and a nylon polo shirt of light beige. The pants were a bit too tight, the shirt showed a little too much bronzed muscle, his hair was just a bit too shaggy and sun-streaked. He was a stunningly handsome man, but his good looks were too calculated for my taste. He looked like a romantic beachcomber, or rather a magazine advertisement's idea of a romantic beachcomber. He should be holding a jar of men's cologne, I thought, or a popular brand of cigarettes. Silly girls and middle-aged women might drool over his good looks, but any sensible woman would steer clear of him.

'You really don't remember, do you, Emmalynn?' he said quietly.

'I—no,' I said. 'What is there to remember?'

He came towards me, strolling casually. He stopped a few feet away from me and rested his hands lightly on his thighs. His lips still curled in that melancholy smile, and his eyes were full of smoky promise. It was a look calculated to disturb, and it disturbed me. I could not look away. I was hypnotized, and he knew it.

'How could you forget?' he asked.

'What are you talking about?'

'You were so lonely,' he said. 'The old woman kept you confined, and there was no one to talk to, no one to understand how you felt. Besides me. You were afraid at first—afraid of me, afraid the old woman would find out. You were stiff and proper and cold—at first. And then—'

'I don't believe you,' I said firmly. 'I—I may not remember, but I know myself—'

He shook his head. 'You thought you did. You ignored me. You refused to talk to me—stiff and polite and imperious—at first. But all the time you were curious, and your curiosity finally broke you down.'

I stared at the man, disbelieving. He implied that he had made love to me. It was very logical—I was lonely, repressed, and he was available, ready to welcome me. Anyone who didn't know me would find it easy to believe. Certainly any woman would find it easy to believe. Boyd Devlon spoke in a persuasive voice, sincerely.

'That's why I didn't leave,' he said softly. 'I kept hoping you would come back. After—after she died I wanted to move on. I wanted to forget all about this place, but I couldn't. There was always the hope that you would return, and you did—a stranger.'

I said nothing. The sun glittered on his hair, and his eyes were sad. He looked boyish and vulnerable now, an actor in a television soap opera who has been deserted by his one true love. I could not imagine myself in those arms. I could not imagine myself kissing those large sensual lips or stroking that shaggy hair that curled on the back of his neck. Dr Clarkson once told me that people never know themselves. They know the person they want to be, but the real person lurks inside, never recognized, feared.

'Must we be strangers?' he asked.

'I'm afraid so, Boyd,' I replied.

'Until you remember?' he asked, his voice husky.

'I—until I remember.'

'Then?'

'Then we'll see,' I replied.

'You will remember? The doctor thinks so?'

'Yes. That's one of the reasons I came. He thinks being here will help me remember—everything. It won't be pleasant, but I'll be cured.'

'Until then I'm an employee,' he said, shaking his head, 'a stranger who works for you. I guess I'll have to accept that.'

'I'm afraid you will.'

He grinned, the melancholy lover vanishing immediately. 'Well, there's hope at least,' he said. 'And we can be friends in the meantime?'

'Of course,' I said. I smiled nervously.

'Fine. That's better than nothing. Is there anything you want me to do this morning?'

'No.'

'I think I'll bring the Rolls out and wash

it and wax it. It'll keep me busy, and maybe when you see it like it was—it'll help. Maybe you'll let me drive you somewhere. I'll put on the uniform and you can sit in the back seat, like you used to. You might remember something.'

'Perhaps. You never know.'

He nodded, brisk and confident now.

'Where are the keys to the car? They weren't given to me. I had no idea it would be mine. The will said the estate and everything on it—I suppose that included the car.'

'I've got them,' he replied, 'upstairs. I always kept them, and no one asked me for them after it happened. I'll run up and get them.'

He went back up the stairs and came down in a moment with the keys. He backed the old car out of the garage and parked it on the drive. He brought out a hose and a rag and a can of wax. I watched idly as he began to wash the Rolls. The dingy grey surface began to gleam after he soaped it down and washed all the dirt and dust away. He pointed the hose in the air and let the water splutter down. Streams of soapy water rolled off the car and soaked into the drive. Boyd Devlon worked quickly, effectively, with no apparent effort. There were several things I wanted to ask him. I waited until he had dried the car and was beginning to rub wax on the now gleaming body.

'When did you start to work for Henrietta?' I asked, trying to sound casual.

'I started a few days after you moved in here.'

'Did you apply for the job?'

He shook his head, busily spreading the wax over the roof of the car. 'She phoned me, said she needed a chauffeur and caretaker. I was living in Brighton, working on the docks.'

'She knew you? I never heard her mention you.'

'She knew my father quite well, I understand. She kept in touch with him until he died, and she remembered me. Sent me a birthday card now and then. She even came to visit me once when I was at Oxford—eight years or so ago. We lost touch after that.'

'You went to Oxford—and you were working on the docks?'

'I dropped out after the first year. Too stuffy for me, too many books and not enough action. Green lawns, bells tolling, dignified old buildings, not my sort of thing. I joined the navy, and after that I just bummed around.'

'Surely you could have found a good job?'

'Surely. I could have put on a suit and a tie and a tight collar and worked in a nice, calm office. There were plenty of my father's old classmates who were willing to hire me, but that wasn't my sort of thing. I was too restless—so I just knocked about.'

'What did you do?'

'You really want to know? I worked as a bouncer in a Marseilles clip joint for a while, and I went to Kimberley and worked in the mines hoping to get hold of a few diamonds myself. Worked as a waiter in Cannes, and on the crew of a rich man's yacht, came back to London, delivered groceries for a restaurant firm—you name it, I did it. I finally came to Brighton and became a stevedore—'

It was very romantic, exactly the kind of history Billie would have furnished for him. I wondered how much of it were true, if any. Perhaps I was not being fair to him. Perhaps he had done all the things he claimed to have done. It was a little too much like slick magazine fiction to convince me. Working as a chauffeur for a rich, temperamental old woman would fit perfectly into the pattern. I simply couldn't imagine a man wasting himself like that, but then I didn't have Billie's romantic idealism. I was far too realistic to find any of this attractive.

'You found the body, didn't you?' I asked.

'Yeah,' he replied casually. 'I'd been in Brighton drinking with some buddies. She always let me take the car when I wanted to go out for a bit. I stayed at the bar, drinking, throwing darts, talking to the girls, and it was a lot later than I thought. I came home about three and found her. Called the police immediately. They asked me where I'd been of course, and I told them. They checked with my buddies. They asked me if I had any idea who did it, and of course I told them about Reed.'

'She had been quarrelling with him, hadn't she?'

'She made him stop building that extra room. He was plenty mad about that. He threatened to kill her. He was in a dive drinking away and talking about her and calling her names, and he said he'd get even if it was the last thing he did. The police arrested him immediately. Open and shut case, even before they found the axe.'

'It must have been terrible for you, finding her that way.'

'I've seen some ugly things in my time,' he said grimly, 'but never anything to match that.'

'And you stayed on here? I don't see how you could have.'

'They needed someone. For a couple of weeks the place was swarming with people—reporters, police, but most of all curiosity seekers. They all came to look at the place, came right up on the porch and peered into the windows, looked for souvenirs. If I hadn't been here they'd have torn the place apart. I was stationed out front with a shotgun for the first couple of weeks—had to drive them away.'

'Did anyone try to break in?' I asked.

'Plenty tried. I kept them all away.'

'And after it all died down? After the newspapers dropped it? Did people still come?'

'A few. People have a morbid curiosity. They were mostly youngsters, come to look at the bloodstains, come to be frightened. No one's been about for weeks now, though. New sensations take the place of old ones.'

He had applied wax all over the car now, and he stood back to let it dry. It turned hard and flaky as it dried, a streaked pink powder covering the glittering dove grey. Boyd jammed the rag in his pocket and stuck his hands in his hip pockets, leaning back against the car. It was warming up now, the chilly breeze gone, the sun rising high. There were a few beads of perspiration on his forehead.

'Are you familiar with the house—the rooms?' I asked.

He nodded. 'Sure,' he said.

'Which room did Mrs Stern stay in?'

'On the second floor, right hand side, third

from the front. It's all done up in blue and grey, I believe.'

'Is there anything particular about the room?'

'How do you mean?'

'Anything that looks unusual.'

'Not that I know of.' He paused. 'Come to think of it, there's a stuffed eagle on the wardrobe. She was an eccentric old dame, as you well know. I suppose she thought it amusing to have an eagle watching over her as she slept.'

'Did the police search the house after the crime?'

'They went through it pretty thoroughly, thinking they might find some kind of evidence. Not that they needed any. There was no question about who did it.'

'They searched her room?'

'I suppose so. They were here for about three days, going over everything.'

That explained the shredded wallpaper and the torn chair, I thought. I might have imagined everything else about last night, but I hadn't imagined that the room had been searched. That was the one thing I had been sure of. The police searched the room, looking for evidence. It had been searched months ago. Why had I imagined someone had just left it? Why had I felt the paper had just been shredded, the stuffing pulled out of the chair just a few minutes before I entered the room? The feeling had been there, but I had imagined it. The police pulled the furniture out. The police left the room untidy. Another mystery explained.

'Did Gordon Stuart come to the house?' I inquired.

'Yes, about three weeks after it happened. The will was being held in court at the time, although it was pretty certain Stuart would inherit the place. I had orders to let no one in, and no one meant Stuart as well. He was pretty angry when I refused to let him look over the place, threatened to have me discharged, but Mrs Stern's lawyers had given me the job and I knew they were the ones who'd have to fire me. He went away in a fury. As far as I know he never came back. Wait a minute—' He frowned, his eyes turned inward, reflecting on something he remembered.

'No,' he muttered to himself, 'that wasn't Stuart—'

'What is it?' I asked.

'One night I thought I heard something around at the side of the house and went to investigate. There are six French windows in the parlour, you know. They all open directly on the veranda. That was where the noise had come from. The windows were all closed, apparently locked, but I noticed one of them was loose. I pulled on the handle and it came right open. The fasteners were all old, of course, rusty, but this one looked like it had been tampered with. The window might have been forced open, someone might have explored the house and then tried to fix the window back so that it would seem locked. I went through the house. There was no sign of anyone's having been there, but I had a feeling—just the funny kind of feeling you get sometimes. I had the feeling someone had been looking around, though I couldn't prove it.'

'You thought it might have been Gordon?'

'At first. He swore the house was his and that he'd get in, no matter what I said. At first I thought it might have been Stuart, then I changed my mind.'

'Why? Did you see someone else?'

'Not then. I hung around outside, and after a while I saw someone on the beach, walking along in the moonlight. It was Reed—George Reed. He was walking back towards his cottage, that damn dog of his following him. He could have just been restless, unable to sleep, taking a stroll, but it was the middle of the night and a little too coincidental to suit me. I was suspicious.'

'Of George Reed? Why?'

'I'd had a couple of run-ins with him before about his trying to get into the house. We had words more than once. I almost slugged him one night. I was on the veranda and saw him sneaking around and told him to get off the property. He challenged me. We almost fought.'

'Why did he want to get into the house?'

'He said he wanted to find proof that his father didn't kill her. He's been making a nuisance of himself ever since it happened. He says he knows his old man didn't do it and claims he's going to prove it. People around here are getting pretty tired of him.'

'I suppose his reaction is normal,' I remarked. 'No child would like to believe anything like that about one of their parents.' I shook my head. 'I guess it'll be hard on him when—when I remember. I'll have to make a report to the police, of course, and when I tell them what I saw he won't be able to cling to any more illusions about his father.'

Boyd Devlon stared at me for a long moment without speaking. He seemed to be pondering something very serious, his brows creased, his mouth tight and turned down at one corner.

'Emmalynn,' he said, his voice heavy, 'you stay away from Reed. You hear?'

'Why—whatever do you mean?'

'Stay away from him,' he repeated.

Something in his tone caused me to shiver. His eyes were hard, and he was frowning. He reached up to brush a bleached lock of hair from his forehead. He looked suddenly formidable, almost dangerous.

'I can't think of any reason why I should have dealings with him,' I said, 'but why should I stay away from him?'

'I don't like him. I don't like him at all.'

'Is that any reason why I should feel the same way?' I asked lightly.

Boyd looked at me sharply. His hands were clenched into tight fists. He looked as though he wanted to knock someone down, sturdy, bull-like, his anger temporarily banishing the casual confident young man who was poised and relaxed. He was a different person now, and I was alarmed.

'What's wrong?' I asked.

He sighed deeply. He relaxed. He took the rag out of his pocket and began to rub the hardened wax off the car.

'Nothing—' he said, his voice casual once more. 'Forget it. I have no right to bring it up—'

'Bring what up?'

'Reed—George Reed. Look—promise me

you'll avoid him.'

'Very well—but why?'

He put the rag down and faced me. He was calm now, but that steel-like anger was still there, carefully controlled.

'When Henrietta had her lawyer stop old Reed from building he was mad, like I said, and he threatened to kill her, and everyone assumed he did. I don't doubt it myself. But if they hadn't found the axe and if it hadn't had the old man's fingerprints on it, I'd have sworn George Reed did it instead of his father. Old Reed was angry, and he talked a lot when he'd been drinking, but talk like that is usually just an outlet. Whoever killed Henrietta had to be unbalanced—insane. I can't feature an old man like Reed committing such a crime, but I can see his son doing it.'

'What makes you say that?'

'The father was a loud mouthed old cuss, but he was simple, doing his work, drinking too much, never bothering anyone. His son is one of these angry young men you're always reading about—hard, intolerant always trying to stir things up. He's smart, got a lot of schooling behind him, and he was always writing editorials about the rights of the people and the injustices of the rich and that sort of thing. When Henrietta put his father down like she did he was seething mad. Not loud and outspoken about it like his old man, but seething. It was just another example of injustice as far as he was concerned, and you could see his anger, tight lips, cold eyes, belligerent attitude. I'd have put my money on him for the murder right away.'

'But you didn't say anything about this to the police?'

'It was just a feeling I had. I saw her body and I thought he's done it, he's killed her. And then when they asked me about it I knew it was just my own feeling and I couldn't very well explain it. The old man had threatened her. That was something definite to go on. As it turned out he was guilty after all and it was just as well I didn't mention the other. I hadn't been able to shake the thought, though. I saw the body, and immediately I thought of George Reed.'

He heaved his shoulders and turned back to the car. He rubbed the wax from the surface, revealing patches of gleaming dove grey beneath the pink chalk. 'Reed's up to no good,' he said. 'He's a troublemaker. I don't want anything to happen to you.' He said this last lightly, looking at me with smiling eyes. 'I want you to get well. I want you to remember.'

I nodded briskly and turned to leave. I didn't

want to start back on that particular line of conversation.

'Will you want a drive this afternoon?' he asked.

'I—I have to go for groceries. You can drive me to the store. Shall we say one o'clock?'

'I'll have the car around in front, waiting.'

I hurried away. Boyd Devlon went back to waxing the car. The sun was sparkling now, bright yellow. I circled the drive around to the front of the house. The water was blue-white, sweeping in large waves over the sand. I paused for a moment, looking at it, and then I strolled down the shaggy green lawn towards the boathouse, walking slowly, thinking about the things Boyd Devlon had told me. I wondered how much of it was true. I wondered how much I should trust a man who was so obviously after something, and I wondered just exactly what it was he was after.

CHAPTER SEVEN

It surprised me that the boathouse hadn't been torn down. It was merely an eyesore now, the old roof rotting, the window panes broken and the paint long since peeled off the sides. The water slapped against it. Barnacles clung to the boards near the water level and dried salt crusted the wood in glittering particles. It was large enough to hold several boats. I doubted that it had been used in years. An old row boat was overturned in the sand near the boathouse, a gaping hole in its bottom. A rotten fishing net hung on poles beside it, and coils of old rope hung on nails beside the door. I stepped through the door, curious to see what the inside of the boathouse looked like.

Sunlight came through the broken windows but it was immediately transformed into an aqueous green light that wavered on the walls. A ray touched the water and sent shimmering silver reflections on the ceiling. The smell was overwhelming, moss and water and dead fish and rotting rope. There was a wooden walkway around three sides of the place, a railing protecting it, and the rest was water that slapped gently against the wood. To my surprise there was a boat tied up to the railing, a sixteen foot motor boat with a tiny cabin. The motor was crusted with rust, and the red and white paint on the body hung in dry shreds. Some old cushions were piled in back of the boat beside a rusted anchor and a coil of rope.

There was something eerie about the place. I couldn't discern exactly what it was, but it was there, almost tangible. The horrible smell, the water slapping against the wood, the greenish light, the ruined boat: all combined to give me a feeling of uneasiness. Outside there was sunshine and fresh air, but here there was only decay. I shuddered, standing at the railing and looking down at the murky water. The silver reflection shimmered, the water slapped, the boat bobbed on the water, its prow scraping against the wood. I heard something rustling, and the sound startled me. It did not belong. Rats? Not so near the water. I leaned forward, listening, trying to identify the sound.

My fingers gripped the rotting railing. I looked down at the water. I heard the rustling sound again, and then I felt a chill stealing over me. Someone was watching me. The sensation was acute, real, as real as the horrible odour, as real as the noise. I could feel a pair of eyes staring at me. I whirled around. The door I had come through hung half open, but no one was there. Sunlight sifted through the windows with their jagged edges of glass, and no shadow fell across them, yet even as I searched I felt the eyes on me. Then I heard a giggle.

It was a soft sound, but unmistakably a giggle, half smothered by a hand held over the mouth. My knees felt weak. I gripped the railing, terrified. I wanted to tear out of the boathouse, but I was too frightened to move. The sound came from the boat. I peered at it, and through the dirt streaked windshield I could see a shadowy face, a pair of eyes watching me. The rustling noise came again, followed by another giggle. I remembered the soft laughter I had heard—or thought I heard—last night on the stairs. The boat rocked. Someone was climbing out of it. I was petrified.

I closed my eyes. My heart was pounding violently, and I was breathing heavily. There was another giggle. I remembered a television show I had seen where the homicidal maniac giggled before plunging a butcher knife into his victim's throat. I could see the fuzzy black and white picture in my mind, flickering on the tiny screen, and I thought I would pass out. I felt my knees buckle a little, and I gripped the railing to keep from falling. This was it, I thought. Burt Reed didn't do it after all—the killer is here, coming towards me. Open your eyes. Look.

'Scared-ja, didn't I?'

A child scampered over the prow of the boat and swung over the railing to land on the walkway a few feet from me. I backed against the wall, my heart still pounding. I looked at the tiny creature with the grin smeared across her dirty face. Relief came in great waves, and anger came with it. I wiped a strand of hair from my temple. My hand trembled visibly.

'Who *are* you?' I whispered hoarsely.

'Betty's th' name, Betty Murphy, I scared-ja, didn't I?'

'You're a wretched little girl!'

'I know. Ain't it awful? Everyone says that. I'm a terrible pest and a horrid child, sure, but I don't give a slip about what all them flippin' people say.'

'What were you doing in that boat?'

'Spyin'.'

'Well, you had no business there. You—you don't belong here. Where *do* you belong?'

'I belong at th' store. I mean, that's where I'm suppos'ta be, but my ol' lady, my Ma, she's so busy she ain't got time to watch after me and I go just 'bout wherever I wanna go—'

She paused, peering up at me. 'I know you,' she said. 'I remember you. You're Miss Em'lynn, ain't-ja?'

'That's right. Do—do I know you?'

'You usta live here, right? 'N you usta sometimes come to th' store 'n buy groceries, before the old lady was chopped up. You bought a chocolate bar one time 'n then pretended you didn't want it and gave it to me. My ol' lady didn't like that. She clouted me on the side of the head, but I kept the chocolate.'

I was calmer now, the fright gone, the anger gradually disappearing. A few minutes ago I would have gladly tossed the creature into the water and thrown rocks at her as she tried to climb out, but now I felt slightly more gracious. I took her hand and dragged her out of the boathouse. The sunshine was blinding after the dim green glow inside. I examined the child.

She was a tiny thing, scrawny, with long legs and thin arms, a young colt covered with dirt. Her white-blonde hair was cut in short ragged locks that framed her perfect heart-shaped face. Her eyes were a lively brown, with long curling lashes, and golden freckles were scattered across the bridge of her turned-up nose. Her mouth was bow-shaped, vividly pink. Beneath the streaks of dirt I could see that her thin cheeks were rosy. She wore tennis shoes and a pair of tattered blue jeans that bagged a little in the rear and a red and white striped T-shirt that had obviously belonged to someone else at one time. She looked the rugged little tomboy, but she was an appealing little waif just the same. Her brown eyes sparkled, and there was a hesitant smile on her lips. She stood with her hands jammed in her jeans pockets, her chin tilted defiantly. My anger melted away, but I was determined to be firm nevertheless.

'Do you always go around spying on people?' I said sharply.

'Sure. That's my hobby. You see, we ain't got television 'n there ain't nothin' else to do around here. I see lots of things. I know more 'n anyone around here. I *see* things. It's better'n television any day!'

'You should be spanked,' I snapped.

'Ain't no one I know who's big enough,' the child said nastily.

'I am,' I retorted.

'You ain't either. 'Sides, you're too pretty.'

'You think so?'

'Yeah, you sure are. Particularly now. You used to be just as pretty, 'course, but you wore your hair all pulled back and fastened in a bun, and you didn't ever wear anything like whatja got on now. The old lady would have busted a gut if you'd-a worn a skirt that short.'

'What do you know about—about her?'

'Plenty. I know plenty.'

'How?'

'I told-ja. I spy. Plenty of times I usta look in the windows, 'n I'd watch both of ya. She run me off once—I was hidin' behind a chair on th' veranda and lookin' in the window. She was primpin' in the mirror, makin' faces at herself and smilin', 'n I couldn't help but laugh. She saw me and screeched like she'd been stuck with a pin. Then she came tearin' out after me. I ran like hell!'

'Nice little girls don't use words like that.'

'I ain't a nice little girl. Where'd-ja get that idea?'

'How old are you?'

'Ten and a half.'

'Why aren't you in school?'

'It's Saturday. 'Sides, I play hookey all the time. They can't keep me there.' She paused, her head cocked to one side. 'I *hate* school,' she added.

'Why?'

' 'Cause Old Barney—Miss Barnes—is always payin' attention to Priscilla Sue 'n bein' sweet to her 'n not givin' a *damn* about me. She says I'm a bad influence on Priscilla 'n all the other kids.'

There was something plaintive in the child's voice, and for a moment she was sad and vulnerable, all the pretentious wickedness gone. Her mother was a widow and ran the local store, I knew, and Widow Murphy was probably much too busy to give the child proper care and attention. Betty reminded me of a little lost kitten, but I knew if I tried to cuddle or stroke her she would screech and claw like an alley cat.

'Are you really so mean?' I asked.

'I'm mean as hell.'

'I don't think so,' I said.

She looked startled. 'You don't?' she said. She sounded disappointed, staring up at me with incredulous brown eyes.

'I think you just pretend to be so people will pay attention to you,' I said, my voice severe.

'You got any kids?' she asked saucily.

'Of course not.'

'Then don't be so smarty 'n try to figure me out. Dr Smith tried to. He is one of them—whatjacall'em? Counsellors? He talks to kids at school 'n I had several sessions with 'im 'n he said I was really a sweet little girl who needed love and a stable home life. Know what *I* said?'

'What?'

'I said *crap!* I got ten demerits for that,' she

added proudly.

I stared at her, trying hard not to laugh. 'If you're such a horrid little girl, I don't need to waste time talking with you. You'd better go home. I'll find someone not quite so wicked to talk with.'

Betty frowned, her brown eyes showing first resentment, then disappointment. Her shoulders drooped and she looked like she had just been slapped. Her ragged blonde hair hung limply about her face, and she reached up to wipe a streak of dirt from her chin. 'Maybe I'm not so wicked,' she said quietly, 'least not to people who're nice to me. You usta be nice. I remember th' chocolate bar. I'm sorry I scared-ja, Miss Em'lynn. I heard you'd come back 'n I wanted to see if it was true so I sneaked off and came here first thing this mornin', just to see you. I didn't mean to scare ya.' She looked up at me with that hesitant smile.

'I'll tell you what,' I said. 'I wanted to take a walk this morning. Why don't we walk down the beach towards your house? Your mother is probably worrying about you. Is it far?'

'The store? We live behind th' store. No, it's 'bout a mile if you go along th' beach. If you're drivin' it's twice as far.'

'Come along then,' I said briskly.

We walked down the beach, away from the

boathouse. Betty scampered in the sand, a little ahead of me, stopping now and then to examine a shell or a piece of driftwood. The breeze blew my hair and whipped my skirt, and the water swept over the sand and shingles. I wanted to take off my shoes and stockings and wade in the water, but I knew I had to maintain a certain dignity with the child. Soon we were far away from the boathouse, walking along a desolate stretch of beach that seemed to extend for miles and miles with no sign of human habitation. The beach was flat, the white sand glittering in the sunlight, and the ground beyond it rose up in huge dunes that were covered with tall brown grass. A seagull circled over the water and cried out loudly. Betty was several yards ahead of me. She stopped to let me catch up with her.

'Mind if I ask you somethin'?' she said.

'Of course not,' I replied.

I stopped to take off my shoe and shake the sand out of it. Betty sat down on a large piece of driftwood, hesitant about asking her question. She dug the toe of her tennis shoe in the sand, not looking at me.

'Are you crazy?' she asked.

I was dumbfounded. 'Why—no! Why do you ask that?'

'I just wondered—' She picked up a small

rock and sent it sailing out over the water. 'I didn't *think* you were, but they said you couldn't remember nothin', and people who can't remember are looney. Everybody knows that. They say you don't remember bein' here. Is that true?'

I nodded.

'You didn't remember *me*, and you used to be so nice. You were always smilin' at me and speakin' soft 'n all. I didn't *want* to believe you were crazy. I'm glad you're not. Even if you can't remember, I'm glad you're not crazy. I kinda wanted a friend.'

'I'd kinda like a friend myself,' I replied, my voice quite serious. 'Everyone needs to have someone to talk to—even when they grow up and get to be as old as I am.'

'What about that man?' she asked. 'Can't you talk to him?'

'What man?'

'Th' one you were kissin'. Don't tell me you don't remember *that*?'

'I—uh—I'm afraid not,' I said carefully. 'Why don't you tell me about it.'

'It was a long time ago, before th' old lady was killed. It was late 'n I'd been makin' my rounds and was goin' home. I saw you standin' on the beach, lookin' real lonely, and then the man came out and and you talked for a long time 'n then he kissed you and you put your arms around him. I was hidin' behind a sand dune and I stepped on a rock and made a noise and you two jumped and looked around real nervous like and then I ran away. Ya didn't ever see me.'

'Are you quite sure about this?'

' 'Course.'

'Who—who was the man?'

'Well, it was gettin' dark, and his back was to me 'n I never saw his face, but he had broad shoulders, ya know? 'N muscles, 'n he was wearin' blue jeans and a T-shirt. I wouldn't let no one kiss *me*. I'd knock their teeth out if they even tried.'

We were silent for a while. Betty had picked up a stick and was making pictures in the sand. I stood looking out over the water, watching the blue grey waves sweep over the sand. Far away, along the horizon, the water was darker, merging into a deep purple line against the misty sky. I wondered what else this child might have seen in her 'spying.'

'I got somethin' to show you,' Betty said.

She reached into her pocket and took out a tiny piece of wood, holding it carefully in the palm of her hand. She held it up for me to examine and I saw that it was a small dog, beautifully carved in miniature, every detail perfect.

It had been done by a craftsman, an artist. I asked her where she got it, and Betty looked sad. She was silent for a moment, looking at the carved dog, and I thought she might cry. Then she frowned and put the piece of wood back into her pocket.

'*He* gave it to me,' she said, 'th' one they said done it. I told him gee I wish I hadda dog 'n he sat right down and took out his knife and made it for me then 'n there. He made a boat for Sean, too—Sean's my brother. He was such a nice old man. I played checkers with him lots of times in his cottage, but he cheated. I was just a kid 'n he didn't think I'd catch him, but I did. He just grinned 'n said I was too smart for 'im.'

'You—you're talking about Burt Reed?'

'Sure. He was always promisin' to take me fishin' with him. He was goin' to, he kept sayin', 'n I bet he would of it they hadn't taken him off to jail like that.'

I held my breath. I didn't move. She continued to speak.

She spoke quite calmly, her voice almost philosophical. 'He wasn't a bad man,' she said. 'I know that. I know he wasn't—' She looked up at me, her eyes suddenly grave. 'I know somethin',' she said. 'I wanted to tell it before, but I was 'fraid to—' She hesitated.

'Then he died and there wasn't any need to—'

My heart began to pound slowly. Betty frowned.

'That night—' she began, her voice hesitant.

'What—what do you know?' I whispered.

I must have seemed too anxious, too eager to know. Betty paused, and she searched my face. I knew she had been on the verge of telling me something important, but I could see her drawing back now. She tightened her lips and narrowed her eyes, and her tiny hands clutched the edge of the piece of driftwood she was sitting on.

'Please tell me,' I said. 'What do you know?'

'I know plenty,' she said, nodding her head, 'but I ain't gonna tell. I didn't *then*, 'n I sure as hell ain't goin' to now.'

'Betty—'

'I seen somethin'—'

'Don't you trust me? Can't you tell me?'

She shook her head. 'Nope. I'm 'fraid. That man tried to get me to talk—his son. He knew I was always hangin' around and he tried to make me talk, but I didn't. I kept my mouth shut. I'm afraid of 'im. I ain't sayin' nothin'—Ma told me not to.'

'You told your mother?'

'Sure, 'n she was scared, too. She said it wouldn't do no good to go 'round blabbin' 'bout somethin' you couldn't prove, 'n I'm just a kid and everyone'd think I was lyin' because he was my friend and gave me the dog. He was a nice old man, though. I'll tell you that. He didn't—'

She paused. Her face was pale, the brown eyes enormous. She seemed to be remembering something.

'Betty—' I said quietly, trying to contain my excitement. 'If—if you know something, and you could prove he was a nice old man and didn't do what—what they say he did, you should tell the police. It could mean a great deal.'

Betty got off the driftwood and kicked her heels in the sand. 'Yeah, I could be chopped up just like th' old lady. That's what it could mean, 'n I ain't about to run that risk.' She looked at me sharply. 'I shouldn't-a said nothin'. Ma warned me to keep my mouth shut.'

'You don't trust me?'

'I don't trust no one. You mighta done it yourself.'

'Betty!'

'I—I'm sorry, Miss Em'lynn. I didn't mean that.'

I knew I would get no more out of her at the present time.

'Look,' she said, 'there's Sean. He must be comin' after me.'

I turned to peer down the beach.

The boy was walking slowly towards us. He was perhaps fourteen, tall and lanky with deeply tanned skin and unruly hair that was not quite blond, not quite red. He wore tennis shoes and a pair of blue jeans cut off above the knee. His sleeveless brown and yellow jersey was ragged. As he came nearer I could see the grave expression on his young face, a crease between his brows, his brown eyes solemn. He was a handsome lad, but there was something disturbing about him. It was as though he had never had a childhood, as though he had been forced into manhood before he had had a chance to be a boy.

Betty seized my hand. 'Don't say nothin',' she pleaded in a hurried voice. 'I—I was fibbin'. I didn't see nothin'. Don't mention it. Sean will tell Ma 'n she'll give me a hidin'—'

The boy stopped a few feet away from us. He did not even look at me. He was frowning deeply. Betty released my hand and went over to him.

'Here I am,' she said brightly. 'You lookin' for me?'

'Ma's been worried. I told her you'd just

gone out to play, but she was worried. You know why.'

'I was just makin' my rounds.'

'I've warned you about that,' he said grimly. 'You're going to get into serious trouble one of these days.'

'I wasn't hurtin' nothin'—' Betty protested.

The boy took her hand, and he looked at me for the first time. 'What lies has she been telling you?' he said.

'Why—she's told me nothing.'

He looked down at his sister, apparently satisfied.

'Come on, then,' he said. 'We've got work to do.'

The children walked on down the beach, away from me. Betty turned to give me a quick wave before they disappeared behind a sand dune. I felt my pulses leap. I pressed my fingertips against my temples and tried to drive the ugly thoughts from my mind. The waves crashed loudly. A seagull cried overhead, and it sounded like a scream of anguish. I looked around at the barren sand and the bleak sand dunes. The sun was hot, burning down on this emptiness. I felt like I was the lone survivor after a world catastrophe, and I was afraid. I turned and began to hurry back the way we had come. I hurried away from the desolate stretch of beach, away from the emptiness, away from the terror that had gripped me as I listened to the words spoken so earnestly by that highly unusual child.

CHAPTER EIGHT

It was almost noon. I wandered among the gardens at the side of the house. They had once been lovely, no doubt, but now they were overgrown with weeds and thorns, only a few of the rose bushes blooming. A grey flagstone path wound around flowerbeds, clumps of shrubbery, ending at a pond in the middle of the gardens. It was white concrete, cracked, and dead leaves floated on the surface of the dark green water. A white marble nymph stood in the centre of the pond holding aloft a broken jug from which water must once have poured. There was something melancholy about these gardens, enclosed by thick black trees at back and side. The nymph stood lonely sentinel, her dead white eyes peering out over tangles of dark green leaves that hid most of the white and yellow roses.

I stood by the pond and looked up at the towering old house. The blue roof sloped and rose in several levels, the turrets and gables throwing dark shadows over the blue shingles. The windows stared down darkly like evil eyes. It was a hideous monstrosity of a house with its weathered grey sides, jutting corners and spreading wings crouching beside the ocean and guarding so many dark, ugly secrets. I wished I was in Clive's studio, helping him photograph bizarre models against bizarre backdrops. I wished I was in noisy crowded London with its fog and confusion, and its raucous celebration of life. Here there was only silence and gloom, and an evil pall that hung over the place even now when the sky was blinding white and sunlight poured down in wavering yellow rays.

It's just a house, I told myself, just a place. The evil is in your mind. I could not shake the fear that lurked inside me. It had been there from the very first, but it had grown even stronger since I had listened to the child talking in her fierce little voice. She had seen something, she said. She knew something. She was afraid to tell. What could it be? Why did I feel a chill as I walked over the cracked grey flagstones and touched the dark green leaves and watched a small brown lizard scurry over the path and disappear in the black soil? It would be best to leave now, to give the whole thing up. I had thought myself strong enough and brave enough to go through with it, but now I wasn't so sure. I didn't think I could spend another night in the house.

Billie came out on the veranda and stood on the steps. She was wearing an orange and white shift and her hair was pulled back in a pony tail, tied with an orange ribbon.

'Lunch!' she called gaily. 'I've brought it out here. The dining room is much too grim!'

'Marvellous,' I called, trying to sound enthusiastic.

'Why, Em—' she said. 'You're pale. What's wrong?'

'Nothing. The heat—'

'It's not hot.'

'Isn't it? The—the gardens are so grim.'

'Spooky is the word,' she replied lightly. 'The whole place is spooky, if you ask me. I've been exploring this morning while you've been on your mysterious errands. Both the wings are absolutely layered with dust, all the furniture covered with white sheets and cobwebs stretching from corner to corner. Come on—' She led me up the steps and onto the veranda. 'There are cucumber sandwiches, if you wish to believe it! And iced tea. Why he bought *cucumbers* is beyond me!'

The veranda was cool and shady, heavy vines dangling from the eaves of its roof and shielding us from most of the sun. There was a wooden table and three chairs painted orange and an old porch rocker covered with worn brown velvet, its plump cushions smelling of dust and camphor. A yellow paperback French novel had been left on the rocker, its pages limp and crumbling, and a bouquet of white roses had been dropped behind it, long since withered. A tea tray set on the table.

I sat down on the rocker and examined the book. Billie poured the tea and handed me a sandwich.

'Just think,' she said, 'you might have been reading that novel, and you might have left it out here—you do read French, don't you?—and someone might have given you the roses. Perhaps Boyd Devlon.'

'He doesn't strike me as the type who'd give a girl flowers. He's more likely to hit her over the head and drag her to his lair.'

'You think so?' she inquired, delighted with the idea.

'This is Henrietta's book. She loved these sexy things. I would read the classics to her, and she'd read these on the sly. She loved roses, always had them around.'

'It's a creepy feeling, isn't it? Sitting here, knowing she was here just a few months ago. Thank God I don't believe in ghosts—not *really*, I mean. It's strange to go through rooms and know she was there, to step out on the front veranda and know that's where it happened—'

'I know,' I replied quietly.

'It must be even worse for you, Em. Have you remembered anything?'

'No. It's all still hazy.'

'Hazy? But that's marvellous! There was *nothing* before, a blank, and now it's hazy. Oh, Em, I just know you're going to start remembering before long. You've been acting so strangely.'

'Strangely?'

'Last night—prowling around in the dark. And a few minutes ago. When I first came out you looked—well, terrified, in broad daylight, and you were pale, dear. What happened?'

'Nothing—really. Just—just a child.'

'A child?'

'She was in the boathouse. A little girl—Betty Murphy.'

'What on earth was she doing in the boathouse?'

'Spying,' I replied.

Billie put down her sandwich and stared at

me, one brow lifted. She was wearing a pale orange lipstick, and her lids were delicately shadowed with brown. Her nails were painted bright orange, and she wore several gold bangle bracelets on one wrist.

'Would you care to *explain* that?' she said.

I told her about Betty Murphy. I told her everything the child said, leaving out only the reference to the mysterious man I was supposed to have kissed on the beach. I spoke slowly, trying to remember the exact words the child had used, and Billie listened with a serious expression on her face. She nodded once or twice, her enormous brown eyes sparkling, and I could tell she wanted to interrupt me. When I finished she sipped her tea, looking down at the table, a slight frown creasing her brows.

'It scares me,' she said.

'I know.'

'I'm serious. It scares me.'

I nodded.

'I've read everything about the case, Em. You know that. Some girls work crossword puzzles, I play Sherlock Holmes and try to solve baffling crimes. It's been a game—great fun, looking at the bloodstains, being pleasantly frightened, reading all the articles and forming my own theory. It's been a lark, like visiting a haunted house, but—it's not a game anymore.'

I didn't say anything. I sat back on the dusty brown velvet cushions and looked out at the gardens. The sunlight was no longer quite so bright. Small clouds were forming in the sky, and the sky was slowly turning grey. The wind rattled the vines that hung from the eaves.

'You could be in serious danger,' Billie said quietly.

'I don't really think so, Billie.'

'I have something to show you,' she said.

'Do you? What?'

'I'll run get it.'

She went inside the house and returned a few minutes later, bringing a pulpy magazine which looked like a supplement of a Sunday newspaper. The papers were crumpled and were turning yellow at the edges. Billie opened it and folded it back at an article. She handed it to me.

'Read it,' she said.

A HOMICIDAL MANIAC? The title was two inches high, seizing the reader's attention with brazen effectiveness. There was a picture of Burt Reed. His face was weathered and wrinkled, but the thick lips were grinning, and the eyes seemed to sparkle with mischief. It was an innocent face, almost childlike, the lines pleasant, the kind of face most people would trust immediately. The article began with a blow-by-blow description of the murder, sparing no details, and then gave a short history of the man's life, showing the incongruity of such a life with such a crime. Next there were comments by people who had known Reed. All of them expressed shock and disbelief that he could have done such a thing. They mentioned his salty wit, his fondness of children, his love of the sea. There followed brief accounts of famous crimes committed by seemingly normal people who would never have been suspected of such heinous behaviour. The article ended by saying that the police had dropped the case, although Reed had never been officially convicted of the crime. DID HE DO IT? the author asked in bold black letters. At the bottom of the page there was a sketch of an axe, red ink splattered all over the margins of the paper.

'What a foul piece of journalism,' I said.

'It's grisy, but it does pose a question.'

'Not seriously, Billie. It was written to cater to the minds of uneducated people who'd get a vicarious thrill out of believing a maniac was still on the loose. I—I'm convinced Burt Reed did it.'

'Really, Em? Do you really believe that?'

'The—the police arrested him. They found the axe. It had his fingerprints on it. They were sure he did it.'

'But he died before they could *prove* it.'

'Em, they're underpaid and overworked. They had what *appeared* to be an open and shut case. The public was satisfied. No one complained besides Reed's son and that was perfectly natural. They dropped the case because everything seemed to fit so well and there didn't seem to be any reason to keep on with it. They searched the house. They found no clues. Burt Reed fit perfectly. He had a strong motive. He had threatened to kill her. The axe was found behind his cottage. The threat and the axe were the only two concrete things they had against him.'

'Rather enough, I think. After all—'

'Burt Reed was an amiable man who liked to drink, and when he drank he talked big. He had too many one night and was shooting off his mouth, and said he was going to kill the old witch. Was that really a threat, or was it merely an old man letting off steam after he'd had too much? I know I have said some pretty cutting things in anger that would certainly put me in a suspicious light if the person I was talking about was suddenly murdered. I think the police put too much emphasis on the threat.'

'What about the axe?'

'Simple. He kept it in his shed. Naturally it would have his fingerprints on it. Someone with gloves on could steal it, use it and then hide it under the shrubbery. When it was found, it would have her blood on it and his fingerprints—but not the prints of the real murderer. Anyone who has read a few detective stories could figure that one out.'

'You're very convincing.'

'Em—this particular murder was done by someone out of their mind. It was the crime of a madman, a maniac. Look at Reed's picture. Do you really believe he could have done it?'

'I don't know.'

'That child—'

'She could have been lying,' I said.

'She could have, but if she wasn't—she may know something vastly important.'

'She's just a child.'

'That's right. No one would pay any real attention to her. *You* are the only one who knows for sure. That's what scares me, Em.'

'If—if Reed didn't do it, then—'

'Who did?' she asked flatly.

We were silent for a moment. Billie seemed to be on the verge of saying something. She glanced at me, frowned, then tapped her fingernail on the table top. Her brown eyes were filled with worry. She was much more subdued than she ordinarily was, and I could tell that something was on her mind, something she was keeping from me. She crossed her legs. Her gold bangle bracelets jangled noisily as she moved her hand. She finally sighed deeply, hesitated for a second and then spoke.

'Em—'

'Yes?'

'I—I have something to tell you.'

'What?'

'I don't know if I should. I don't want to worry you—Em.'

'Tell me.'

'I found that magazine in one of the rooms this morning.'

'Why should that worry me?'

'The room was closed up, dusty, but there were three cigarette butts on the floor and the magazine. It—it's dated two months after the murder. Whoever had it, whoever was reading it had no business in the house. The place was shut up, waiting to be turned over to whoever inherited it. Someone was in that room—someone who had no business being there.'

'Perhaps it was Boyd Devlon,' I said.

'That's what I thought at first, but then I saw the cigarette butts. Boyd Devlon doesn't smoke. He mentioned it last night. Em, it was frightening. There I was in that room with all the dust and cobwebs and the white sheets over all the furniture, and I had the strangest feeling that someone had just left, that someone had walked out just before I came in. I could almost *feel* someone watching me.'

I looked away from her. The sky was darkening rapidly now.

'Billie,' I said seriously, 'do you want to leave?'

'I—don't know. I don't *think* I'm a coward.'

'We can, you know. We can go back to London this afternoon.'

'I hate to give up,' she replied. 'Em, I feel that somewhere in this house there's a clue—something that will point to the real murderer. Of course, Burt Reed probably did it and we're probably being hysterical women and acting like idiots, but I've never had the kind of feeling I had this morning in that room. Do *you* want to leave?'

'I think not,' I said calmly. 'I ran away once. I don't want to run away again. If I left now, I might never remember. But—Billie, I think you should leave. You can take Clive's car and go back to London. If there is some kind of danger, I don't want you involved.'

'You want me to leave?' she asked.

'Yes,' I said. My eyes were grave.

'And leave you here alone? Not on your life.'

'But—'

'We're in this together, Em,' she said.

I took her hand. I squeezed it. After a moment we smiled.

'Just the same,' Billie said. 'I'm glad Boyd Devlon's around.'

'Me, too,' I said. I glanced at my watch. 'He's supposed to be around front at one. It's almost that time. He's going to drive me to the store in the Rolls. It's mine, incidently.'

'A Rolls Royce?'

'The genuine article.'

'You don't mean it?'

Billie closed her eyes dramatically.

'Touch me quick,' she said. 'I've never known anyone who had a Rolls. Think what a smash it'll make back in London.'

We stood up, the moment of tension vanished now. We walked around the veranda to the front of the house. I tried not to look at the place where the floorboards were dark with stain. I stared at the sky. It was grey now, growing darker. Clouds were massing on the horizon, and a mist had rolled over the water. There was a distant rumble of thunder. I knew that sudden changes in the weather were not at all unusual on the coast, but it seemed hard to believe that the sun had been sparkling less than an hour ago. Boyd Devlon wasn't out front yet. I sat down on the steps, watching the wind torment the water. The waves were choppy, angry, capped with foam.

'Do you want to go to the store with me?' I asked.

'I don't think so. I'll stick around here.'

'I wonder where Boyd is?'

'Em, look!'

She pointed towards the boathouse. A beautiful rust red dog was romping along the beach, prancing in the sand, evidently waiting for someone to catch up with him. He saw us and barked, then loped up the lawn towards us, stopping a few feet away and wagging his long tail, wanting some encouragement before coming closer. His fur was long and glossy, his lines thoroughbred. He looked at me with large brown eyes. I whistled. He charged up to the steps and laid his head in my lap, whining ecstatically.

'Hello, Nelson,' I said, scratching his head.

'Em—' Billie said, her voice full of excitement.

'Yes?' I looked up, startled.

'You called his name!'

'Did I?'

'You called him Nelson. You know him. He knows you—that's obvious. He came right to you.'

'Well—'

'You remembered his name,' she whispered. 'It's happening just the way Dr Clarkson said it would. Little things would come back first, he said, and then bit by bit you would remember.'

'Nelson?' I said. 'Did I say that? Are you Nelson?' I asked, rubbing the dog behind the ear. He licked my hand and whined, sad and happy at the same time.

'It's *his* dog,' she said. 'Remember? It ran out and barked at the car yesterday when we were passing the cottage. It's his dog, and there *he* is!' She pointed to where George Reed was walking down the beach, drawing near to the boathouse.

He stopped and whistled, looking around for the dog. He was of medium height, rather stocky, with powerful legs and arms and enormous shoulders. His hair was dark and he wore glasses, but he was too far away for me to discern any features other than the stocky, athletic build. He wore a pair of tennis shoes without socks and tight white jeans that encased the strong well-moulded legs. His white shirt was open at the throat, and the sleeves were rolled up over the immense biceps. From this distance he looked like a Roman gladiator in incongruous modern dress.

He called the dog's name, then he turned towards the house and saw us on the veranda.

He hesitated for a moment, his fists on his thighs, staring at us. The dog barked once and wagged its tail but made no effort to join its master. I stroked the animal's fur, watching as George Reed came slowly up the lawn towards us. He stopped perhaps fifteen yards from where I was sitting on the steps, and he glared at us, not speaking.

His face was crude and Slavic with a square jaw and high, flat cheekbones. His mouth was wide, the lips a little too thick, and his nose was large, slightly crooked. There were dark smudges beneath his brown eyes. They stared from behind the heavy, horn-rimmed glasses with intense belligerence. His dark brown hair was coarse, parted severely to one side, lying flat against the skull. The face was almost ugly, but strong character was stamped in every line. There was no refinement there, no grace, but there was a fierce, rugged vitality about the man that was apparent in his every gesture, and he emanated strength and vigour to an almost overwhelming degree.

'So you've come back,' he said. His voice was menacing.

'Yes.' I replied. My own voice quivered nervously.

'That was a very foolish thing to do,' George Reed said.

CHAPTER NINE

He stood there with his legs planted wide apart, his fists resting on his thighs, his pose an exaggeration of masculine dominance. His head was lowered, his brows arched, his wide lips turned down at one corner. I thought he resembled an incompetent actor trying to portray a gangster in a cheap film. His posture was a little too melodramatic, his voice just a bit too menacing to ring true. I rose slowly to my feet, my expression challenging him. Billie huddled behind the railing, staring at the man with undisguised fascination. He looked like a truck driver or a blacksmith, but there was an obvious intelligence in the savage brown eyes. The man had been to medical school, and from all reports he had been brilliant. He couldn't possibly be the coarse peasant he appeared to be.

'Why shouldn't I have come back?' I asked crisply.

'You know very well.'

'I'm afraid I don't.'

'They're saying you have amnesia, that you don't remember being here. Is that true?'

'Yes, it is.' I retorted.

'You don't remember me?'

'I'm sure the memory would be an unpleasant one if I did,' I said.

He smiled a little at that in spite of himself, then he grew all grim and menacing again. I was suddenly reminded of an irate little boy defending his rights. In that brief, flickering smile I had seen a charm that, under other circumstances, might be most attractive. I understood why he was studying to be a doctor. There was something of the crusader about the man. He would be passionate and idealistic, ready to save the world, ready to knock down anybody who tried to stop him. He would have mercurial temperament and he would be capable of a whole range of emotions that most men could only simulate.

George Reed's father had been arrested for a heinous crime, and the son believed him innocent. Ever since the murder he had been protesting his father's innocence, loudly and belligerently, and if he had a chip on his shoulder it was perfectly understandable. I found myself justifying his animosity. Still, at this moment he was a threatening figure standing there with the scowl on his face. He looked dangerous, capable of murder himself, and I stepped back a little, remembering what Boyd Devlon had said.

'Your amnesia must be very convenient,' George Reed said harshly.

'What do you mean by that?'

'There are certain things it would be convenient not to remember. You may be able to fool some of them, but you can't fool me so easily. You may be very clever, Miss Rogers, but—'

At that moment Boyd Devlon drove the car around the side of the house and parked it in front. He opened the door and got out slowly, staring at George Reed with an expression almost as menacing as the one Reed himself wore. The two men glared at each other. I could feel the enmity in the air. It was like a strong electrical current charging between the two of them. Boyd stood by the car, his back rigid, his jaw thrust out, and Reed leaned forward a little, tense, ready to hurl himself at his enemy and pummel him with those tight fists. There was another rumble of thunder, nearer this time, and the sky was dark grey. It seemed to stain the earth and rob it of all colour.

The dog leaped down the steps and pranced around its master. It seemed to sense the tension, stopping, growing rigid, whining loudly.

I watched the two men in the vague grey light, both so still, both so tense, and it was like a curious black and white photograph of two combatants. A strong wind blew over the water, ruffling their hair.

'Get out of here, Reed,' Boyd said slowly. His voice was flat.

'You think you can make me?' Reed retorted. Once again I was reminded of a sullen little boy.

'I think so,' Boyd said. He moved away from the car, taking a few steps toward Reed. He stopped, took a deep breath and heaved his shoulders. Reed didn't move but I could see him tighten up, ready to spring. I gave a gasp.

All that fury was about to explode. Both men were ready to punish and pound. I could almost hear a fuse hissing, burning closer and closer to the stick of dynamite. I was terrified.

I moved quickly down the steps. I stood between the two men. Both of them ignored me. I was caught in the crosscurrent of animosity. I could feel it radiating from each of them.

'No, Boyd,' I said.

'Get out of the way, Emmalynn,' he said gruffly.

I flushed. I turned to face George Reed.

'Please,' I said quietly.

George Reed stared at me for a long second,

his dark brown eyes filled with conflicting emotions.

'Please,' I repeated. He sighed and relaxed, and he shook his head as though to clear it of the rage that had possessed him so thoroughly. He snapped his fingers at the dog and then turned around and walked down the lawn towards the beach, his head held high, his back proud. I knew it had been hard for him to give in like that, particularly to a woman. He walked along the beach, the dog prancing behind him, and soon he was out of sight.

Boyd was still angry, his handsome face hard. He was wearing his uniform, slender beige pants and a beige jacket that fit tightly about chest and shoulders, brass buttons down the front. He looked like the door man at some chic restaurant. I found the uniform slightly ludicrous under the present circumstances. It would suit Henrietta's fancy to have him dress like that, turning a proud man into a glamorous toy. I wondered how a man with his obvious assets could submit to what was really a subtle kind of mockery. The Rolls Royce gleamed behind him, gorgeous now with its polish and style.

'You should have let him handle him,' he said.

'And what would you have done?'

'I'd have beaten him to a pulp.'

'Really? And that would have solved something? You men are always so ready to fight. It must be something in your nature—a craving for violence. I just don't understand.'

He didn't say anything. His face was sullen now, as though he had been cheated out of some anticipated pleasure. I smiled wryly, shaking my head I told him I had to go inside for my purse and would join him in a few minutes. He rubbed his jaw, his eyes lowered. Billie and I went back into the house.

'I thought they were going to kill each other,' Billie whispered as we walked down the hall.

'It was all very stupid,' I replied.

We went into the parlour, where I had left my purse.

'He's fantastic,' Billie said. 'George Reed, I mean. He'd as soon knock you down as look at you. I've never seen anyone so belligerent. I kept asking myself if he was for real. He seemed so larger than life, like he was really shy and sensitive and just pretending to be so rugged.'

'I got the same impression,' I said.

'I felt sorry for him, I don't know why exactly. It must be horrible to know everyone thinks your father did something so hideous and to believe him innocent. I can understand why he's so fierce, but still—there was something about him—'

'What do you mean?'

'I don't know if I can explain it. I was sympathetic, despite his arrogance and animosity, but I got the impression that, well, that he would be quite capable of murder himself.'

'Did you?'

'I was actually frightened before Boyd came. I thought Reed was going to come up the steps and tear you limb from limb. Em, what on earth did he mean about your amnesia being "convenient"? It was almost as though he suspected *you* of killing her.'

'I suppose everyone's a suspect to him,' I replied casually, picking up my purse and checking to see that everything was inside.

'You remembered the dog's name,' she said. 'I wonder how you knew it in the first place? The dog came right to you, as though you were an old friend. Reed seemed to know you pretty well, too.'

'Perhaps he did,' I said vaguely.

'O, Em, it must be *hell* not to know. But you remembered—the veil lifting. You'll start remembering more and more.'

'That's what frightens me,' I said.

We walked down the hall towards the front door. The light outside was getting darker and darker, the sky a drab grey now, black clouds forming. We stepped out on the veranda. Boyd was sitting in the front seat of the Rolls, his arm curled around the steering wheel.

'It's gorgeous,' Billie said, indicating the Rolls. 'So is Boyd, in that uniform. Why on earth is he wearing it now? It's just a little out of place, don't you think?'

'He seems to think it will help me remember. He always wore the uniform when he drove me on shopping expeditions, he said. Is there anything you want from the store?'

Billie shook her head. Boyd insisted that I get in the back seat of the car. I felt slightly ill at ease as we drove away. The motor purred with a pleasant hum, and the car smelled of wax and polish. He had cleaned the interior, too, and the red leather was soft and pliant. I stared at the back of his head, unable to think of anything to say. The hair curled about his thick neck in small wisps. The heavy beige cloth of his jacket stretched tightly across his shoulders. We rode in silence, Boyd, the proper, subservient chauffeur. It was a role completely out of character with the man as I believed him to be.

We passed through the wooded area that surrounded the house then drove onto the main road that climbed up from the beach and paralleled it, going beside steep grey cliffs that dropped down to the water's edge. I watched the white-capped waves crashing against the great grey jagged rocks that stood like grotesque bathers in the edge of the water. Plumes of foam spewed up, lashing at the rocks. The scene had a certain barbaric grandeur, but it was somehow depressing. We drove for perhaps two miles then took a side road that wound back down towards the ocean, passing great clumps of dark green shrubbery that seemed to grow out of the face of the rocks that rose up on either side of the road.

'How far is Brighton?' I asked.

'The city's about five miles on down the road.'

'Where are we going now?'

'It's a resort area, a little community spread out over the beach for people who can't afford the more splendid accommodations of the city. Widow Murphy has her store there. It's about a mile from the house, though we've driven twice that far to get there by road.'

'That's what Betty told me.'

'Betty?'

'The widow's little girl. I met her this morning.'

'Did you?' His voice was cool and casual.

'You know her?' I asked.

'Is she the kid who's always snooping around?'

'Probably. She was in the boathouse this morning. Spying, she said.'

'What else did she say?'

'Several things—very interesting. Most of them lies, probably.'

'I've run her off the place a couple of times,' Boyd said. 'Once she was hiding in the garage, and one time I caught her trying to break into the house. She's a nuisance, has no business hanging around like that. It would be so easy for an accident to happen—'

We completed our descent and drove along a large paved road that ran along the beach. On one side of the road small houses and cottages rose up in tiers over the sloping hill we had just come down. They were brown and grey and pink, and most of them looked deserted now that it was out of season. On the other side of the road there was a flat, sandy beach and dozens of small shops, many closed, painted yellow and brown and grey. Besides the shops there were wharfs and piers with tied-up boats bobbing in the choppy water. There was a deserted swimming area with a tall yellow platform for the lifeguard and an enormous casino with crumbling pink plaster walls and broken windows. It was all scenic and sad, kind of cut-rate Riviera for bank clerks and factory workers who wanted to spend their short vacations by the sea.

Widow Murphy's store was situated on a large wharf built out over the water. There were sea shells and fish nets in the front windows, and behind the store there was a large pen area with railing where one could sit in the sun on pleasant days or fish or watch the boats. Boyd parked the Rolls on the crushed shell parking area beside the store. He opened the door for me, nodding politely, his face expressionless. As I went into the store I could see him lounging against the car, the patient chauffeur waiting on his employer. I was rather irritated by his manner. He seemed to be mocking me in a subtle kind of way, wearing his uniform, insisting that I ride in the back seat, treating me with a distant coolness that wasn't at all what I would have expected after this morning.

There didn't seem to be anyone in the store. I took one of the pushcarts and began to fill it with various items, moving down the long rows of food displayed in neat stacks. Besides food there were paperback books, a display of sun tan oil with a huge cardboard cut out of a statuesque blonde with improbable brown skin, sea shells, sun hats, beach balls, everything a summer visitor might wish. I had almost finished my shopping when Widow Murphy came out from a room in back. She was a small, thin woman with faded blonde hair and wrinkles about her worried brown eyes. One could read the history of her life in that face with its tightly stretched skin and sharply defined bones. It was a history of hard work and tragedy. One could see that she seldom smiled, forced by necessity into a hard, taciturn mould, and one knew instinctively that she was both honest and severe.

She stood behind the counter waiting for me to finish my shopping. She nodded once but gave no other sign of recognition. Her dark brown eyes were filled with suspicion, and I felt strangely uncomfortable as I finished a hurried selection. She checked me out without a word. Young Sean came out from the back of the store to sack the groceries and carry them out to the car. She rang the money up on the cash register and gave me my change. I was curiously moved by this grim woman who wasn't too many years older than I. I wanted to say something comforting to her, but I didn't know what to say without sounding patronizing. I stepped outside.

Boyd was still lounging against the Rolls, his arms folded across his chest, his eyes narrowed, watching Betty Murphy talking with great animation to Gordon Stuart, whose car was parked on the other side of the store. I paused, startled to see Gordon here. I was immediately on the defensive, knowing his presence here was no coincidence. Betty was holding something up in her palm, showing it to him, and he bent down to examine it, a smile on his lips. He looked up and saw me. He patted Betty on the head and came over to where I was standing in front of the door.

'Hello, Emmalynn,' he said casually. 'I stopped by the house to see you, and your attractive friend told me you'd left for the store. I thought I'd try to catch you here.'

'What do you want?'

'I just want to talk with you for a few minutes.'

'I'm in a hurry—'

'Surely you can spare a few minutes,' he replied in that curious voice that was both coarse and silken smooth.

'Very well,' I said. I wanted to know what Betty had been saying and I felt a rather wicked satisfaction in having Boyd see me with another man. Gordon smiled faintly, pleased at this easy victory.

He wrapped his hand around my elbow and led me to the area behind the store. The hard wooden planks extended far out over the water and we could hear it surging below us. I stood at the railing, the wind whipping my hair about my face. The sky was grey, enormous black clouds along the horizon, and the light was dim, everything tinged with grey. I wondered how long it would be before the storm came and unleashed all this fury. Gordon stood beside me. He wore a pair of narrow brown slacks and sportcoat with a subdued pattern of brown and dull gold checks. His tie was dark gold silk, and he smelled of expensive, leathery male cologne. His short steel grey hair was cut in flat, tight locks over his skull. This affluent gloss contrasted with the lean, hard buccaneer's face with its sharp lines and heavy arched black brows.

'I notice you were talking with Betty,' I said.

'An unusual child. Most unusual. Quite precocious.'

'You think so?'

'Definitely. She has very unusual habits. She's quite a talker, too. She told me about meeting you this morning, and she showed me a wooden dog she claims Burt Reed made for her.'

'Oh?'

'An interesting child,' he said. 'Starved for affection, of course. She was prowling around the car, peering through the windows, and I smiled at her and started a whole flood of conversation. Your beautiful young man seemed quite interested in what she was saying. Of course she was talking loudly enough for him to hear.'

'I wouldn't put too much stock in anything she might have said,' I replied. 'She's very imaginative.'

'So it would seem.' He paused, his eyes studying my face. 'I didn't come here to discuss children,' he said quietly.

'What did you come for?'

'I came to apologize for yesterday. I feel I was rude. I'm afraid I may have left an unpleasant impression.'

'You certainly did,' I replied stiffly.

Gordon Stuart shook his head slowly, as though in regret. He looked into my eyes, and his own had a hypnotic effect on me. Many years ago I had been a complete slave to his magnetic charm, and I had been hurt. Now I was still fascinated, as one might be fascinated by a cobra.

'You look extremely attractive with your flushed cheeks and windblown hair,' he said. 'It's a shame this is the twentieth century. Two hundred years ago you would have been a king's prize possession, glorified in furs and velvet.

'And you, no doubt, would have been a pirate,' I replied, playing along with him.

He nodded, smiling. 'I would have kidnapped you and taken you off in my ship. I would have beaten you into subjection, and then I would have given you the world. Today, alas, I must humour you and use gentle persuasion in order to get my way.'

'Very fanciful talk,' I said crisply. 'Six years ago I would have been intrigued.'

'Six years ago I made a dreadful mistake,' Gordon replied. 'I hope there's some way to remedy it.'

'There's no way,' I said.

'Do you hate me so very much?'

'I feel nothing—one way or the other.'

'Ah, but you do—' he said smoothly.

'You think so?'

'You don't know yourself—as I know you.'

His blue eyes turned smoky, the lids drooping seductively at the corners. 'We had some nice times back then. Remember?'

'I try not to think of them.'

'You were such an eager pupil, and I was a skilled instructor, showing you how to break out of your shell of timidity, showing you how to feel things. You were so incredibly naive, and I was so patient.'

'And you got what you wanted—money.'

'Do you think that's all I was after?'

'Perhaps you wanted a—a bonus,' I said icily.

'Had I wanted it, had I really intended to hurt you—'

'I find this very tiresome, Gordon.'

'I've never been able to forget you, Emmalynn,' he said. 'I won't pretend there haven't been other women since, several of them, but I've never been able to forget those weeks. I've often wished to recapture them.'

'There is no way to do that, Gordon.'

'There are ways,' he whispered huskily.

He slid his arm around my waist and pulled me to him. He wrapped his fingers about my chin and raised my face to his. There was a dark glitter in his eyes as his lips moved over mine. He held me loosely, and his mouth pressed and probed and sought some sign of response. He swung me around in his arms, and his hand moved down to my throat, the thumb gently pressing the pulse. It was a long, expert kiss, strangely passionless, calculated to stir the most primitive emotions. There was a tight smile of triumph on his lips when he released me. The smile died slowly when he saw that I had been entirely unmoved.

I was almost amused by the man's incredible ego, an ego that permitted him to believe he could overwhelm me with that one skilful kiss.

No doubt it had been effective many times before on many other women, but I knew him or what he was, and I was immune to his polished skill as lover of women. I had an impulse to smash his face with the palm of my hand, but that would have given him too much satisfaction. I raised my hand and wiped it slowly across my mouth. That wounded him.

Gordon didn't say anything for a moment. He was rigid with anger, his lean body tense. I could see the anger crackling in his blue eyes. It took him a moment to gain control of himself, and when he spoke his voice was as hard as steel.

'Very well,' he said, 'we'll have to play it another way.'

'So it would seem.'

'I intend to have the house, Emmalynn.'

'You may as well give up, Gordon.'

'I had hoped this could all be pleasant and profitable for both of us. I can see I was mistaken, but—no harm trying. I didn't want to use heavy artillery but it seems I'll have to.'

'Oh? Are you going to have me committed?'

'I wasn't joking about that yesterday. It would be very easy with the right doctors paid to say the right thing. I've already made a few discreet inquiries into the matter.'

'You're wasting your time, Gordon. I promise you that.'

He shook his head. 'I think not.'

'I don't know why you want the house, but I promise you you won't get it.'

'I'll get it,' he said, 'one way or another.'

'There's no way.'

'If something were to happen to you, My Dear, the house would be mine immediately. I wouldn't have to wait around for a bunch of doctors to declare you legally incompetent. Mmm—' He stroked his lower lip, contemplating something. 'An accident perhaps,' he continued. 'All sorts of accidents could happen.'

'I'm very careful,' I said.

'An accident could be—arranged.'

'Oh, come off it,' I said impatiently. 'You sound like the villain in some shoddy television show. If you think you're frightening me, you're very much mistaken.'

'Am I?'

I was standing with my back to the railing. Gordon moved a step closer to me, his body almost touching mine, and I had to lean back to look up at him. He was smiling, his upper lip stretched over his teeth. He raised his long bony hands and laid them on my shoulders. The strong fingers dug into my flesh. He moved closer, his body against mine, forcing me back. I could feel the railing give way a little. The board creaked. I stared at Gordon Stuart, my face calm, my eyes level. It took great control, but I would not let him have the satisfaction of seeing fear in my eyes.

'You enjoy melodrama?' I said.

'It would be so easy—' he whispered. 'So easy.'

'Easier than an axe, perhaps?'

Gordon released me abruptly. He stepped back. He lifted his shoulders in an elegant shrug. I thought his face looked a little ashen, and a muscle in his cheek twitched almost imperceptibly. He did not lose control, but I could see that I had startled him. I straightened up and brushed my skirt. Gordon backed away some more, watching me with a weary expression.

'You stood to gain quite a bit by her death, didn't you?' I said, my voice calm, almost casual.

'You think I killed her?'

'I think you're capable of having done it.'

'You're treading on dangerous ground, Emmalynn—'

'Did you kill her, Gordon?'

'Burt Reed killed her,' he said.

'I'm not so sure.'

'If you're referring to the babbling of that child—' He cut himself short. His face grew guarded.

'Several people aren't satisfied that Reed killed her,' I said. 'But we'll soon know for sure.'

'You sound certain.'

'I am. I remembered something this morning —a little detail, nothing important—but it's coming back. Slowly, but it's coming. Soon I'll remember everything.'

'Perhaps you won't have the chance,' he said solemnly.

I arched a brow, my eyes on his.

'If Reed didn't kill her, then you're in grave danger,' he said. 'I should think you'd realize that.'

'I'm not afraid, Gordon. Should I be?'

Gordon shrugged again. He tugged at his dull gold tie and straightened the lapels of his sportcoat. The buccaneer's face was composed now, elegant in its lean lines, and the short steel grey hair clung to his head like a tight skull cap. There was a streak of lightning across the grey sky. Gordon glanced up. 'It's going to storm,' he said, his voice polite. 'I suggest we take this up another time.'

'There won't be another time.'

'Emmalynn, do yourself a favour. Leave the house. Leave tonight. Save yourself a lot of unpleasantness. I'm quite charitable, actually. I really don't want to see you hurt. You shall be, I promise, unless you do as I say. Go back to London.'

'Not a chance,' I said.

I smiled briefly and left him standing there. I went around the store to where Boyd stood waiting by the car. He gave me an inquisitive look but didn't say anything. He opened the back door of the Rolls and helped me in. There was another streak of lightning across the sky, and another, fierce silver fingers ripping at the grey, but still the storm didn't come. Boyd got behind the steering wheel and started the car. I saw Gordon walking towards his car as we drove away. His shoulders were hunched forward and his hands were jammed into his pockets. He had a thoughtful look on his face, and he was frowning, as though he had a duty to perform and was reluctant to carry it out.

CHAPTER TEN

I did not recognize the battered blue car that was parked in front of the house. Boyd let me out at the front door and drove on around the back to carry in the groceries. I went inside, curious. I heard voices coming from the library, and as I walked down the hall Billie came out to meet me. She was smiling. Her brown eyes were full of excitement that she could hardly contain. 'I've got something *fantastic* to show you,' she whispered. Her voice and manner were those of a conspirator. 'Unbelievable—' She put her finger to her lips. 'Later,' she said. 'The doctor is here now. When he leaves—'

She ushered me into the library. Dr Clarkson stood up to greet me. He wore brown pants and a rust coloured corduroy jacket with leather patches at the elbows. His silver hair was tumbled on his head, and his blue eyes examined me carefully as I went to shake his hand. He gripped my hand with both his own, holding it firmly as his eyes studied my face. His black horn-rimmed glasses slid forward a little on his large nose, and he nodded his head, apparently satisfied with what he saw.

'Came down for the weekend,' he bellowed. 'Thought I'd better stop by and see how you were. You look radiant. Ah, youth—' He nodded his head some more and released my hand. 'Your friend has been keeping me company. She has the most interesting theories about this crime! The young girls in my day thought about hair ribbons and scrap books, but nowadays it's crime and archaeology and nuclear fission! Can't say as I mind, though. They may not be as feminine as they used to be, but they're a hell of a lot more interesting—the young girls, I mean!'

'Is that a compliment, Doctor?' Billie asked.

'You might say so. Yes, you just might! Emmalynn—' He turned to me. 'Miss Reed here has been telling me that you remembered something today. Is that true?'

I nodded. 'I remembered a dog's name. It just came to me—the name was on my lips. I can't remember knowing it before.'

'The first wedge,' he said, pleased. 'It'll all start coming back now. Still think you can—uh—go through with it?'

'I think I'm strong enough.'

'I know damn well you are! Healthy girl—all young girls today are a healthy lot. Look shiny and underfed and pale, but most of them are karate experts and can fly airplanes and run a mile in seven minutes, that sort of thing. Most unfeminine—most fascinating!'

Billie had, in fact, taken karate lessons and she had done her solo flight in a cub airplane belonging to a former beau. I doubted seriously, however, that she could run a mile in seven minutes unless there was a sale at one of the high fashion shops and no taxi was available. I saw that she had kept the doctor entertained during my absence. I wondered how long he had been here.

'Doctor Clarkson was thoughtful enough to bring gifts,' Billie said. She indicated a bottle of scotch and a box of party mix. 'He was afraid we wouldn't have anything for tea time. It's tea time now—but scotch?'

'Always have it for tea!' Doctor Clarkson exclaimed. 'Picks you up! All these little cakes and fiddle-faddle folks stuff themselves with in the middle of the day—most unhealthy. Disastrous to the digestive system! I am here to tell you that's why folks are so peaked and pale. Cakes! Get us some glasses, girl. Both of you can use a belt!'

Billie went to get the glasses, and Doctor Clarkson and I sat down. He lolled on the vast brown leather couch and I sat on the green leather chair across from him. The library was an enormous room with a vast black marble fireplace and three walls with bookcases towering to the high ceiling. The books were all dark brown and dull gold and red, most of them leather bound and stamped with gold. The fourth wall was composed entirely of tall French windows, all of them open now, the heavy green curtains billowing. There were several dark tables with tall brass lamps with red glass shades. They were old-fashioned oil lamps, and Billie had lighted several of them. Many rich Persian rugs, now old and faded, were scattered over the parquet floor and there was a huge multicoloured globe standing beside the roll top desk.

Doctor Clarkson took out his pipe, and his face sagged a little. The ruddy vitality had vanished as soon as Billie left the room, and he looked at me now with serious blue eyes.

'How is it going?' he asked, his voice low.

'Fine, I think.'

'I'm not so sure about all this,' he said, indicating the house. 'I'm not so sure you should be here.'

'I can't leave now.'

'I can understand why you want to stay, but I'm not so sure I want you have any part of it. There's bound to be a great deal of strain on you. I don't know if you can stand up under it.'

'I'm a healthy girl, remember?'

'I think there might be danger, too, Emmalynn—'

'We knew there would be danger,' I said interrupting him.

'I never seriously doubted that Reed did it,' he said irritably. Doctor Clarkson didn't like to be interrupted. 'If I had thought there'd be any *real* danger, I'd never have agreed to have any part of this. I've discovered a few things I don't like since I saw you last.'

'What things?'

'I've learned something important. This friend of yours—'

'Billie's quite fascinated with the crime. She doesn't think Burt Reed did it. I—I'm not sure I do myself. You can discuss anything in front of her. Anything but—'

He nodded. 'I understand. I know why you want to keep that part of it quiet—for your own good. No one must know, not even your best friend. To be quite frank, I never thought you could carry this off—'

'You underestimate me,' I said.

'You're brave, Emmalynn, too damn brave.'

'Determined, I should say, not brave.'

'Your friend tells me Reed was here.'

'He was. He was—most belligerent.'

'I think he's trying too hard.'

'So do I,' I replied. 'I had an encounter with Gordon Stuart this afternoon. I must tell you about it.'

'What I have to say involves Stuart, too. I can talk freely in front of this girl—up to a point?'

'You can.'

'I wanted to be sure before I said anything. What about this Devlon?'

'He claims I had a love affair with him. He is eager for me to remember so that we can—resume our romance.'

'He's a handsome devil. It would seem likely that you'd have fallen in love with him.'

'It's preposterous,' I said. 'Not me, not with Boyd Devlon. I'm not the kind of girl who falls for bronzed muscles and bedroom eyes.'

'You're quite sure?'

'I'm positive!'

'You never know,' Doctor Clarkson said. There was a twinkle in his eye. 'Given the right circumstances—'

'You can forget that,' I said frostily.

He grinned. 'Ah, Emmalynn, still full of inhibitions. Good girl. I know inhibitions aren't the rage right now what with all this free love and LSD and rebellion, but they're the backbone of the country. Lose them all, and you've lost everything.'

'Sometimes I wonder about myself,' I said. 'I think I must be out of my mind—being here. It's all such a nightmare. Henrietta—I try not to think of her, but I keep seeing it happen over and over again. What a horrible thing to happen, and it's my fault. If I hadn't left her—'

He shook his head, his face grave. 'Don't blame yourself. It would have happened anyway.'

'If only there were some way I could make it up to her.'

'Aren't you doing that now?' he asked quietly. 'Isn't that the real reason you're here?'

'I'm going to find her killer,' I said.

It was out in the open now. I was rather startled that I had said the words. I had tried to convince myself that I believed Burt Reed had killed her. I had tried to pretend that it was all over with, that I had merely come to look over the house before selling it, but I knew now that that was not so. Deep down inside I knew Burt Reed had been innocent, just as his son claimed, and all that had happened since I arrived here only served to strengthen that belief.

Doctor Clarkson didn't make any reply at first. He shifted his large body on the couch and folded his arms across his chest. He held his head down, the silver hair spilling over his forehead, the glasses slipping down on his nose, and his wise blue eyes watched me, noting my anxiety. He was perhaps the one person on earth I felt completely at ease with, the one person with whom I did not have to pretend to be something I wasn't. He was like a father to me, wise, thoughtful, protective, and there was no use trying to hide anything from him.

'I didn't want to come here,' I said. 'I thought it was foolish, a waste of time. I just wanted to sell the house and be done with it. Now I know—I feel—' I made a vague gesture, trying to find the right word to express what I wanted to say.

'I think I know,' he said.

'I *care*,' I said. 'I care, and I want to do something.'

'I admire you for that.'

'Right now I'm scared. I may as well admit it. I'm scared, but I'm not going to give up.'

'You're trying to do too much.'

'There's no one else to do it,' I replied.

'Isn't there?'

'Burt Reed didn't kill her. I can't fool myself into believing that any longer. Too much has happened. I met a child this morning—'

I told the doctor about my encounter with

Betty Murphy. He listened, his head nodding drowsily now and then, his eyelids lowered. I knew from past experience that this was his way of concentrating. He might seem to be on the verge of dropping off to sleep, but he was noting everything I said, and two or three weeks from now he would be able to quote my words verbatim if need be. Billie came in while I was talking. She mixed the drinks and set them out for us. Then she sat down, quiet, subdued, a serious and intelligent look on her face.

'Very interesting,' Doctor Clarkson said when I finished. 'Of course children make things up.'

'I don't think she made this up,' I said. 'I believe her. She was frightened. I could see the fear in her eyes. She knows something, something important.'

'What do you intend to do?' he asked.

'I—I'm not sure. I think I'll go talk to the widow. I think perhaps I can make her see the importance of telling what she knows. Perhaps she'll tell me what she wouldn't reveal to the police.'

He nodded his approval.

'I—I have my own idea about who did it,' I said hesitantly.

'Do you indeed?'

'Yes. I had a most interesting encounter with

Gordon Stuart this afternoon.'

I told them both about the meeting with Gordon. I stepped over to one of the French windows and peered out, looking up at the black sky. The air was wet with mist, and the mist stung my cheeks as I stood there. The dark green curtains billowed around me. Beyond the gardens I could see the black trees bending in the wind, the limbs twisting and snapping. I wandered around the room, running my hand over the spines of the books, touching the cold black marble fireplace, talking all the while, trying to remember all that had been said and to report it accurately.

The doctor finished his drink, and Billie poured another for him. She sat with her legs tucked under her, her hands in her lap, and I could see that she was finding it hard to contain her excitement. There was something she was bursting to tell me, and I wondered vaguely what it could be as I finished relating the conversation I had had with Gordon.

'He threatened you?' Doctor Clarkson asked.
'Very definitely.'
'Hmm. Rather bold of him, under the circumstances.'
'When I asked if he had killed her, he looked stunned—then scared.'
'I can see why,' the doctor replied.

'If only I knew why he wants the house so badly—'

'Ah,' Doctor Clarkson said, smiling grimly. 'I can answer that. Sit down, Emmalynn. All this prowling about gets on my nerves. I've got something to tell you both,' he added, nodding at Billie. 'Emmalynn assures me you're as interested in this as she.'

'Fascinated,' Billie retorted.

'Do you remember Lock?' the doctor asked me.

'Albert Lock, Gordon's lawyer? How could I forget him. He combines all the worst qualities of a grave robber and a professional mourner. He's exactly the kind of man Gordon would have to represent him.'

I sat down in the green leather chair. I picked up the glass of scotch Billie had poured for me. I peered at the amber liquid, swirling it around in the glass.

'There was something about the man that bothered me,' the doctor continued. 'I couldn't say exactly what it was, but something kept revolving in the back of my mind. I seemed to remember reading about him in some rag or other, and I knew what I had read hadn't been flattering. I decided to check up on him. Things were rather slow at the clinic, and I could afford to take off a couple of days.

I turned all my work over to my assistant and started to play detective. It was quite jolly.'

The doctor grinned a rather puckish grin, as though in apology. 'I may not seem the detective type,' he said, 'but I know a lot of people—lawyers, policemen, newspaper journalists. Whenever I want a piece of information I can usually go straight to the man who can get it for me. I asked around about our man Lock, and I found out some rather—juicy, I believe, is the word I want—some rather juicy information about him.'

He paused to light his pipe. He fiddled with the bowl and a match and finally got it to draw. He blew clouds of blue-grey smoke and settled back on the couch.

'I won't go into unnecessary detail,' he said. 'Let it suffice that one of my journalist friends told me something in confidence that would put Mr Lock in a very bad light if it were to be made public knowledge. Armed with that information I went to see Lock.'

'With blackmail in mind?' Billie asked, smiling.

'Call it that if you like. I *had* a piece of information and I *wanted* a piece of information. I felt Mr Lock would be much more cooperative if I had something to bargain with—my silence for his lack of. Did I put that right?'

'Explicitly,' I said.

'What did you find out?' Billie inquired.

'I wanted to know why Gordon Stuart was so all fired anxious to have this house. It didn't jive—that's a good word, isn't it? Jive—it simply didn't jive. Why should he want the house when he had everything else? I knew Lock could provide the answer.'

'And did he?' I asked.

'That he did—and then some. I got quite a reception. Polite blackmail was not even necessary—I was rather relieved on that score. It seems Stuart and Lock had had a falling out when Lock wasn't able to perform the legal miracles Stuart thought he should perform. There was much ill feeling on both sides, and Lock was more than ready to tell me anything I wanted to know about his former employer.'

'Gordon fired him?'

'Yes. The day after I brought Lock to your flat.'

The doctor drew on his pipe and blew some more smoke. It hung in the air in thick blue-grey clouds that curled slowly to the ceiling. The red lamps flickered and spluttered. There was more thunder, more wind. Doctor Clarkson was enjoying himself, deliberately prolonging his account.

'Go on,' I prodded.

'Stuart was in a pretty desperate shape financially when he hired Lock to represent him. He was—still is—on the verge of bankruptcy, and according to Lock the police will shortly be on Stuart's trail if he doesn't get enough money to cover some rather dubious losses. It seems he invested some money that wasn't rightly his—and lost it. When the people he "borrowed" it from find out, there'll be hell to pay. He needs money, and he needs it now. That's why he wants the house.'

'But—wait just a minute,' I said, confused. 'Gordon inherited all of Henrietta's estate besides this house. There should be more than enough to cover any losses.'

'Not a penny,' Doctor Clarkson said abruptly.

'What?'

'A pile of worthless paper. Henrietta's "fortune" was nonexistent. She was worth several million once, but that was many years ago. Little by little those millions leaked away. This house was all she owned. Many people thought it eccentric of her to stay here when she could have stayed at a plush hotel or some chic apartment—she couldn't. When she came back to England she didn't have a shilling.'

'I find that hard to believe,' I said. 'I never suspected—'

'She kept up a grand front. No, you got the house, and Stuart got a pile of worthless paper. It was quite a shock to him, as you can imagine. Quite a shock to everyone concerned. Everyone thought she was loaded.'

'That explains something,' I said, frowning. 'It bothered me that she'd left her entire estate—minus this house—to Gordon. She hated him. She used to rant about him, calling him everything she could think of, and she had a fertile imagination. Leaving the fortune to him didn't fit. Now I can see what she was up to—a malicious prank, typical of Henrietta. It must have given her great pleasure to make the will and visualize his face when he discovered all he'd actually inherited was a pile of paper. It was exactly the sort of thing Henrietta would have relished.'

'I still don't see why he would want this house,' Billie said. 'He couldn't possibly sell it for much.'

'If what you say is so, he wouldn't even have enough to buy it in the first place,' I added.

The doctor held his pipe in the palm of his hand and smiled a sheepish smile. The smoke curled up to the ceiling. Billie and I stared at him and waited for the next comment. I knew it was going to have a punch. I could tell from the twinkle in his blue eyes.

'What do you know about Henrietta's jewellery?' he asked me.

'She had a fabulous collection,' I said. 'She showed it to me once. It was unbelievable. She had—'

'*Had* is the working word,' he replied. 'In the safe deposit box there was a pile of paste, the whole lot not worth fifty pounds. The real jewels had been sold, and there was a written record of each sale. She had been living off her jewellery for years, selling it piece by piece. With the money she got from them she was able to maintain a front. She was able to travel and keep up the pretence, and she fooled everyone. Even you, apparently.'

'She certainly did.'

'Now, here's the interesting part,' the doctor continued. 'Lock and Stuart made a careful study of the sales records for the jewellery, and they compared them with the original inventory of the collection, crossing off each item when they found it had been sold. When they were finished, they discovered that several pieces—the most valuable of the lot—hadn't been accounted for. They hadn't been sold, and they weren't in the safe deposit box. Do you follow me?'

'Of course,' I said.

'Do you see now why Gordon Stuart wants this house?'

'I see,' Billie said.

'You mean he thinks the missing jewels are here?' I asked, startled.

'Indeed I do,' the doctor replied.

'But—that's absurd.'

'My sentiments exactly. Henrietta may have been wildly eccentric, but I can't feature anyone hiding a fortune in jewels in an old house,' Doctor Clarkson said. 'Still, they are unaccounted for, and—to Stuart's way of thinking—it's perfectly logical that they should be here. She had no place else to keep them. She was here the day she died. Consequently, the jewels should still be here.'

'That's not very sound thinking,' I said.

'Stuart is desperate. He's like a drowning man clutching at a straw. The jewels would be his salvation, so he's convinced himself they're here. Unsound, agreed, but perfectly understandable from a psychological standpoint. He *has* to have a straw to clutch, or he'd sink.'

'Who did Henrietta sell the rest of the jewels to?' I asked.

'An English dealer. He has his office in London. Stuart checked with him, and he verified that he had indeed purchased the jewels from her, over a long period of time, piece by piece.'

'Isn't it possible that she could have sold the rest to someone else, someone in Europe, perhaps?'

'There were no records of any other sales.'

'Maybe she didn't keep records. Maybe she sold them hurriedly, on the spot, without going through a lot of red tape. Maybe she needed money immediately and sold the jewels to—to a fence, someone who wouldn't want a written record of the sales.'

Doctor Clarkson nodded. 'You could be right. Henrietta lost her fortune years ago. It's likely that she sold the valuable pieces first, maybe ten or fifteen years ago, without even thinking of keeping a record of it. In her day she was something of a compulsive gambler. Perhaps she sold the jewels to pay gambling debts a long time ago.'

'She used to talk about her gambling days,' I said. 'She'd given it up by the time I came to stay with her, but she loved to recount stories of her nights at the casinos.'

'I'd wager a guess her gambling had a lot to do with the loss of fortune,' Doctor Clarkson replied. 'Anyway, if the jewels are not accounted for, there's bound to be an explanation. *We* may never know what happened to them, but you can safely bet Henrietta disposed of them some way or other, records or no.'

'How much were they worth?' Billie asked.

'They were worth a fortune,' Doctor Clarkson informed us. 'As I said, the most valuable of the lot were not sold—at least weren't sold to the dealer in London: an emerald brooch, a diamond bracelet, a pearl necklace.'

'She gave the pearls to me,' I said.

'That accounts for one item, then,' he replied. 'There are still six other items not accounted for. A ruby pendant—one of the largest rubies in existence.'

'And Gordon actually believes they're hidden here? That's fantastic! It's like something out of Wilkie Collins! *Sane* people don't stuff a fortune in jewels in some desk drawer or shoe box and hope the right person is lucky enough to find them.'

'I doubt if Stuart had too much confidence in his sister's mental stability,' Doctor Clarkson said slowly. 'He probably thinks that's precisely what she would have done with them.'

'He's out of his mind,' I said.

Doctor Clarkson and Billie both looked at me, and I suddenly realized what I had said and the weight it carried. I could feel myself going pale. My hands trembled visibly. I took several swallows of the whiskey. Perhaps he *was* out of his mind. Perhaps he was completely unbalanced....

'That's possible,' the doctor said.

'I didn't mean—'

'Didn't you?'

'I just—'

'This puts a new light on things,' Doctor Clarkson said soberly. 'We don't know that Burt Reed didn't murder her, but we *do* know that Stuart had a whopping good motive. He needed money, needed it enough to kill for it. He still needs it, and he thinks he knows where he can get it.'

'It's incredible,' I whispered.

'Incredible, granted, but true. He thinks the jewels are here, and as long as he thinks that, you're not safe here, either of you.'

I was silent. Billie and I exchanged glances.

'It's up to you, Em,' she said quietly.

'I'm staying,' I replied.

'Very well. I'll stay with you.'

'You're both leaving,' Doctor Clarkson said, his voice firm.

'We're big girls, Doctor,' Billie told him.

'Emmalynn,' he said, gruffly. 'This is nonsense, absolute nonsense. Stuart's interest in the jewels aside, we're all pretty certain Reed didn't kill Henrietta, and if he didn't then there's someone who must be mighty concerned about your memory. This is damn foolishness—no electricity, no telephone—'

'There's Boyd.' I protested.

'That's not enough. You could both be butchered and he wouldn't hear way out there in the carriage house.'

'Nevertheless—'

We all three stood up. The tension in the air was almost tangible. I stood with my arms folded, obstinate, and Billie stood beside me, loyal. Doctor Clarkson glared at both of us, and then he shook his head. He was scowling darkly, his hands jammed in the pockets of his rusty corduroy jacket. He finally shrugged his shoulders and sighed heavily.

'You're stubborn,' he snapped, 'both of you!'

'Sorry,' I said.

'All right. I've got a gun in the glove compartment of my car. I'm going to leave it with you. I hope one of you can use it.'

'I'm a crack shot,' Billie said promptly.

'I'm going back to the cottage now. I've got to stop by and see a few of my local patients—I check up on them every time I come down—and then I'm coming back here. There're dozens of rooms in this house. Since you're hellbent on staying here, I'm damn sure going to stay with you.'

'Really, Doctor—'

'Don't argue with me,' he said irritably.

'Modern women! Damn! Come along now. I'll get the gun.'

We followed Doctor Clarkson out to his car. It was cold, and there was a strong wind coming off the water. The sky was as black as pitch, laden with heavy clouds that rolled ponderously. The doctor took his gun out of the glove compartment, snapped it open to see that it was loaded, snapped it shut and handed it to Billie who took it rather awkwardly by the barrel. Her hand sagged under the weight of it.

'You sure you know how to use that thing?' he barked.

'You want to toss a can up and see me hit it?' she retorted.

'I'll take your word for it,' he said gruffly, climbing into the front seat of the car. 'I'll be back tonight—around nine or ten. 'Til then, be careful.'

'We will,' I said calmly. 'Don't *worry* so.'

'Dammit, Emmalynn, this is serious business.'

'I know,' I replied.

'You should realize—'

'I do,' I said. 'We'll see you tonight.'

He drove away. Billie and I strolled towards the porch, both tired, both relieved that he had finally gone. The sky split open with streaks of jagged lightning and the first drops of rain began to splatter around us in furious volleys. We darted to the veranda. The rain began to pour in savage torrents, and the noise was deafening. We went inside and closed the door. Billie looked down at the gun in her hand, examining it with a great deal of curiosity.

'Do you know how to use it?' I asked her.

'I've never shot one in my life,' she said blithely, 'but I thought I'd better say I could or we'd *never* have gotten rid of him.'

'Billie—'

'Don't scold, Em. I've got something absolutely marvellous to show you. I found them while you were gone to the store.'

CHAPTER ELEVEN

She led me into the library. The rain splattered violently on the veranda, and we hurried to shut the French windows. I closed the heavy green draperies. The room grew dark and isolated, the red lamps glowing with an eerie light. The sound of the rain pounding was unnerving. I had a strong feeling of claustrophobia, as though the walls were slowly closing in on us. Billie stood with her hands on her hips, her eyes full of excitement.

'Do you remember "The Purloined Letter"?' she asked.

'The Poe story? Vaguely.'

'The police searched this house, didn't they? And they found nothing of any particular interest? Well, in the story everyone was looking high and low for a letter, looking everywhere but the most *obvious* place. It was right there before their eyes, in a letter rack—'

'You've found a letter?'

'No,' she said impatiently. 'I was just using that to illustrate. I found something far more interesting. You were gone to the store, and I was bored and tried to read Dostoyevsky and couldn't even begin to get with it, so I thought I'd see if I could find something a little more relaxing, maybe one of those sexy novels you were talking about, in English. I came down here and was browsing around the shelves—such tedious volumes, all either classics or about things like astrology or Egyptian mummies—and I noticed a thin little book with a red leather cover and no title standing right beside a book on azaleas, so I took it down.'

'You're interested in azaleas?'

'Em, you're not listening! I took down the

book without a title. I wondered what it could be—'

'And what was it?'

'A diary, Em! *Her* diary.'

'Henrietta's? But she didn't keep a diary.'

'Oh, but she *did*! Evidently she started it when she arrived here. I was going to read it—think what it might *say*!—when the doctor came. I put it back on the shelf—' She walked over to the wall of books and pulled the slender red volume down. 'I thought you'd want to read it first.'

We heard a door slam somewhere in the back regions of the house. Both of us jumped. Billie dropped the book on a table and picked up the gun. We heard loud footsteps in the hall outside the library, and in a moment Boyd Devlon stepped into the doorway. His hair clung in damp ringlets about his head, and he wore a dripping yellow mackintosh. He raised an eyebrow when he saw the gun. Billie laughed rather nervously. The hand holding the gun was trembling all too visibly.

'Did you intend to shoot someone?' he asked, smiling.

'Not really. I mean—'

'You startled us,' I said.

'Sorry. I thought I'd better come in and see if you needed anything. I put all the groceries away when we got back, but I didn't light the gas stove. If you're going to cook, I'll light it now.'

'Yes,' Billie said, her voice quivering. 'Do. I couldn't possibly manage it after—'

'I'll be in the kitchen if you need me,' Boyd Devlon said. He paused for a second, studying us, his brow still arched. Little rivulets of water dripped down the yellow mackintosh. He left. Billie sighed, looking down at the gun she still gripped with nervous fingers.

'I may not be up to this,' she said.
'Now *you* are pale,' I informed her.
'Really? Am I?'
'As a sheet,' I said.
'I just heard the footsteps and thought—'
'Look, we're both tired. You go on upstairs for a little while. I'll cook dinner. I'm famished myself—cucumber sandwiches aren't very nourishing. We'll eat, and then—'

'What about the diary?' she asked, interrupting me.

'Take it up to my room. We'll read it after dinner.'

'What shall I do with *this*?' She indicated the gun.

'Give it to me,' I said.

I thought this was all taking on elements of a farce. Missing jewels, secret diaries, a violent rain storm, slamming doors, footsteps—it was too much to assimilate all at once. We would feel much better after a good meal. I took the gun from Billie, handed her the diary and prodded her towards the door. I could hear her footsteps clattering down the hall and up the staircase.

I walked over to one of the French windows and pushed back the drapes. I looked out at the gardens, barely visible through the swirling grey mass of rain. Great drops of rain slid over the smooth surface of the window panes, merging into intricate wet patterns. I touched the glass. It was icy cold. I shut my eyes and felt the huge old house closing in on me. I wanted to run. I had come into this of my own volition, but it was too big now, too horrifying.

What had seemed simple and clear-cut had become a maze of confusion. I was trapped in that maze. There are too many elements at work, and I was unable to sort them all out. I had understood, or thought I understood, before, but now I was lost. I had the feeling that there was something terribly important, something urgent that I should know, something I had seen or heard that would provide the key to all this, but I couldn't remember. I wandered in the maze, searching, and that something urgent was just ahead, just out of sight, taunting me.

Remember, remember, my mind said. You saw, you heard, you knew. It was right there... the key. The answer. Something....

I released the drapery. It dropped back in place. I straightened up, throwing my shoulders back, shaking my head slightly. The thing I must do now was maintain calm, stay cool, keep all my senses alert. The time to run had passed. I could not give way to nerves. I couldn't acknowledge the fear that threatened to stymie me. I must keep going. I must cook dinner. I must eat. I must relax. Later. I could think this all out and try to recall whatever it was that plagued me.

The kitchen was in the back part of the house. I walked down the main hall, turned a corner and walked down a smaller hall. It was narrow, the ceiling low, the brown and blue paper peeling from the walls, and I could barely see. The few windows were set high up and little light penetrated. There was an unpleasant sour smell that mingled with the odours of dust and mildewing paper. My footsteps on the bare wooden floor echoed all around me, and it would have been easy to fancy that someone was following me. I glanced over my shoulder. There was nothing behind me but an empty hall, illuminated now by a sudden flash of lightning.

I stepped into the kitchen. It was a large room with dark green walls and a floor covered with brown linoleum. Huge cabinets towered to the ceiling, and pots and pans hung on the wall space not dominated by cabinets. A crude wooden table with chairs to match stood in the middle of the room. I saw Boyd's yellow mackintosh draped over one of the chairs, a bright spot of colour in the dark ugly room. Boyd had just finished lighting the stove. He stood leaning against the zinc drainboard. The big gas stove roared. It was almost as loud as the rain pounding on the roof.

'You *are* cautious, aren't you?' he said.

'What?'

'The gun,' he retorted.

'Oh?' I had hardly been aware of carrying it. I put it on the drainboard and shivered.

'Are you frightened?' Boyd asked.

'I don't really know. I suppose—yes.'

'Why?'

'Burt Reed didn't murder Henrietta.'

'You're positive?'

'Almost. The doctor said—' I hesitated. It would be better to keep that to myself.

'He was here for quite a long time, wasn't he?'

'Yes he was. He's going to come back

tonight. He's going to stay here with us. Just—just to make sure.'

'He doesn't think I'm protection enough?'
'It's not that—'

Boyd smiled, understanding. He moved so that I could get some things out of the cabinet behind him. I put a pot of coffee on the stove, opened a large can of oyster stew and began to slice ham and cheese. I took a red linen tablecloth out of one of the drawers and spread it over the table. It was the colour of blood, the material coarse. I stared at it for a moment, a lovely white cloth soaked in blood, in blood, and I shook my head. What was happening to me? I took down the dishes, brown earthenware with golden daisies painted around the rims of the saucers and plates. I dropped one of the cups. It shattered noisily.

'You're nervous,' Boyd said.
'It's this rain. The noise, the isolation.'
'I'm here,' he said quietly. 'You have nothing to fear.'
'I know it's silly. I know I'm acting like a child.'
'Relax,' he said.
'Shall I set the table for three?'
'I had a sandwich in the apartment. I'm not hungry.'
'Good. I mean—'

'Relax, Emmalynn. You don't have to talk. Just ignore me.'

'You—you're rather hard to ignore,' I said.

'Am I?'

'You know you are. Why—'

'Why what?'

'Nothing.'

'You remember, don't you?'

'Remember what?'

'Us. You and me. I sense it. That's why you're so nervous. You've begun to remember—that's why you're so uneasy, why you dropped the cup. You couldn't really forget, Emmalynn, not completely. That night on the beach when you poured your heart out to me.'

'I can't visualize myself doing that.'

'You did. Believe me.'

'I remember nothing,' I said stiffly.

'When were you last in this kitchen?' he asked abruptly.

'This morning. We had breakfast there.'

'Oh—that explains it.'

'Explains what?' I inquired.

'Why you're so familiar with the room. You seem to know exactly where everything is—the dishes, the tablecloth, the knives. You didn't have to stop and hunt for anything.'

'We examined all the drawers and cabinets this morning.'

'I see. For a moment there I thought—' He paused.

'What did you think, Boyd?'

'I thought it had all come back.'

I was slicing a loaf of French bread. I didn't answer at first. I put the knife aside and piled the bread on one of the earthenware plates. I set the plate on the table, checked to see that the stew was boiling, and then I met his eyes with my own.

'It is coming back,' I said calmly. 'Little by little, bit by bit. I—I'm *letting* it come back. Before I tried too hard. The memory is part of me, in me, but when I make an effort to reach for it, it evades me. I was afraid of it before, but I'm no longer afraid. I *want* to remember and I've stopped fighting it. The fog is lifting, slowly, of its own volition, and things are taking shape.'

'That's good,' he said.

'Being here—just being here helps. Last night I had a dream. I saw the murder. I saw her going down the hall to answer the door. I saw the axe. It was real.'

'And the murderer. Did you see him?'

'Yes,' I said.

He stared at me with questioning eyes.

'A dark shadow, standing there in the shadows of the porch. I couldn't tell who he *was*, but I saw him.'

'Maybe next time you'll be able to identify him,' Boyd said quietly.

'Perhaps. Doctor Clarkson thinks so.'

'This must all be a great strain on you, Emmalynn.'

'It is. I won't try to pretend it isn't.'

'Why are you doing it? Why are you torturing yourself this way?'

'It's something I have to do.'

'A duty to the dead?'

'You might call it that,' I replied.

'I'm afraid I'd call it something else—fear, repression, stupidity, one of those words, maybe all of them. You're afraid of yourself, and you hide behind "duty," an empty word. You did then. You do now. You're missing life—the life you were meant for—and that's stupid.'

'You seem to know quite a lot about me,' I said frostily.

'I do, Emmalynn. I understand you. I may be the only person who has ever really understood you. I know what you want, and I know what you're afraid of.'

'What do I want?' I asked.

'Me,' he said simply.

'And what am I afraid of?'

'Me—and you.'

I didn't laugh. I knew that would have been disastrous. I didn't meet his stare either. I turned my attention to the stew. It was boiling over, filling the air with a delicious aroma. I turned the burner off and poured the stew into two brown bowls. I set the bowls on the table, took out two blood red linen napkins and laid them beside the bowls. Boyd watched me, a petulant curl on his lips.

Everything was ready. I wished Billie would come on down. I felt uneasy in this dark room with this strange man hovering about. The rain had stopped. There was merely a splattering sound as water dripped from eaves. Now that the stove was off there was a heavy silence that was emphasized by the intermittent drip, drip from outside. I poured coffee into the cups. I straightened the silverware and smoothed the blood red tablecloth, and then there was nothing else to do, no other way to fill the long minutes. I had to meet those level blue eyes that studied me so calmly.

'Come away with me,' he said. His voice was low.

'Now?'

'Now. Tonight.'

'Why should I?'

'Because you want to,' he said. 'You want to,' he repeated.

'You actually believe that?' I asked lightly.

'Of course,' he said.

Incredible, I thought.

I smiled wryly. 'I'm a good girl, Boyd. Surprisingly enough, there are a few of us left. I don't go away with men, whether I want to or not. It isn't my style.'

'You think it isn't,' he replied.

He stood there with his arms folded across his chest, the drying hair springing into tight blond-tipped curls, his expression petulant. I wanted to laugh, truly. It would have cleared the air and released the tension I felt. I wanted to tell him he was foolish, absurd, a shop girl's romantic dream materialized, a thing of cardboard and pulp fiction suddenly endowed with flesh and blood, but I knew that he was serious. He took himself seriously, and that was the most amazing thing of all.

'I'm not rich,' I said. 'I'm a working girl. I didn't inherit anything but a broken down old house.'

'What does that have to do with it?'

'Everything, it would seem. I can't afford you, Boyd. I don't know why you thought I could, but I wanted to set the record straight. I'm not good pickings—is that the correct expression?'

'I want you,' he said.

'I'd like to believe I could inspire a grand passion,' I said. 'Really I would, but I'm hardly that naive. I was never in love with you, Boyd, and you were never in love with me. There was nothing between us, nothing whatsoever.'

'How do you know?'

'I sense it.'

'You're deceiving yourself. There was—'

'Besides, Henrietta would never have allowed it.'

'Emmalynn, I've asked you to come away with me.'

'Yes. I'm still trying to puzzle that out.'

'I want to take you away from all this.'

'That's the second offer I've had today,' I replied, keeping it airy. 'It makes a girl feel good. Gordon made a similar offer, though his approach was a bit more direct.'

'You said yourself you didn't believe Burt Reed murdered Henrietta. If that's true, then you're in danger. I want to get you away, before—' He hesitated, his brow creased.

'Before?' I prompted.

'Before it's too late.'

'I see. I'm the damsel in distress, and you want to be the hero and rescue me. Yes, that's it, isn't it? Really, Boyd, you've been reading far too many paperbacks.'

'Emmalynn—' he implored.

'Get real, Boyd,' I said, not unkindly.

'The offer was sincere. I meant it. I won't make it again. A man has his pride.'

'Oh?' I said. The word was a spear thrust.

'I guess I'd better go,' he retorted. 'You don't need me.'

'Well, actually, I don't, now that you mention it. Doctor Clarkson is coming, you see, and—'

'I'll go!' he said sharply.

'What do I owe you?' I inquired sweetly.

'Not a thing. Not a damn thing!'

'At least let me give you a ride to town.'

'I'll walk,' he snapped.

'Boyd,' I said quietly. 'This is all really unnecessary, you know. Be reasonable.'

'I know where I stand,' he said, the outraged male.

He was like a moody child determined to have his way. I decided to let him indulge in drama, walk and be damned. The whole exchange had been absurd, divorced from reality. I wished he were able to see the absurdity of it and laugh as I longed to do, but he was intense and male and his ego had been wounded. I shrugged my shoulders, sorry, but too stubborn to try to reason with him any longer. His jaw was thrust out, his lower lip curled, the blond-tipped curls spilling over his tanned forehead. He slowly moved from his leaning position and let his hand come to rest on his thighs. He spoke in a cool, calm voice.

'I hope you don't regret this, Emmalynn.'

'I hope so, too, Boyd,' I replied, bored with it now.

Billie came tripping into the kitchen. Her high heels clattered on the hard brown linoleum. She had changed into a tight waisted jade green dress with a short full skirt and enormous puffed sleeves. Her tawny gold hair swung free, spilling over her shoulders. 'Food!' she cried. 'I'm ravenous! These people who're always threatening to eat a horse—I won't say I'd go *that* far, but right now I understand the feeling behind the expression.' She noticed Boyd standing by the drainboard. She gave him a little wave. 'You're going to dine with us? Wonderful! I'm glad I changed.'

Boyd stepped briskly across the room and seized his mackintosh up from the chair. He swirled it in the air like a matador's cape and slung it over his shoulder, and then he stalked out of the room. We heard the explosion of noise as he slammed the back door in fury. Billie looked at me, her lips parted, one brow arched inquisitively.

'What was that all about?' she asked.

'You wouldn't believe me if I told you.'

'Try me.'

'Oh, Billie, I was so ugly to him, really, and I didn't intend to be. He was so incredibly absurd I couldn't resist it. Like sticking pins in balloons—you know?'

'Actually I do. But *you*?'

'I couldn't help it. He was so obviously faking it—thinking I would drop everything and run away with him because of his pretty muscles and big blue eyes. He wants to get me away from here. I don't know why. He wants me to leave—tonight. It can't just be concern for my welfare—'

'Curious,' she said.

'He's leaving. Now. He intends to walk to town.'

'Walk? But that's preposterous.'

'I know it is. I offered to drive him, but—'

'Oh well, the exercise will be good for him.'

Billie arranged her lanky body on one of the chairs and put her elbows on the table, extremely philosophical about the whole thing. I wished it were that easy for me to pass it off. I felt remorseful, genuinely sorry I had wounded him and thoroughly perplexed over his reaction. I knew I was going to worry about it.

CHAPTER TWELVE

We were silent. We had finished dinner and were still sitting at the table. There was something sinister about the large, dark kitchen. The rain still dripped outside, and there was an occasional rumble of thunder, far away, receding. I was actively fighting depression, and even Billie had lost her sparkling vivacity. Now that Boyd had gone we were completely alone, and it was not a pleasant sensation. The gigantic old house was still silent, and it seemed to be waiting for an opportunity to swallow us up. I tried not to think of all those dark dusty rooms and the long narrow corridors thronging with shadows and soft noises, but I didn't seem to be able to think of anything else.

'Hitchcock would love this place,' Billie said.
'Wouldn't he? Did you see *Pscyho?*'
'Unfortunately. Three times.'
'I wonder if Boyd has really gone?' I said.
'I wonder when Doctor Clarkson is going to be here,' she retorted. 'I am not really a coward, but—' She reached across the table

and took hold of my hand. Her face pale. I was startled and started to ask her what was wrong, then I heard the noise too. It was coming from the front part of the house, a frantic pounding noise.

'What—' Billie began.

'Someone is pounding on the front door.'

'But who?'

'We'll soon find out,' I said sharply. 'Come on.'

We left the kitchen and hurried down the narrow halls. I led the way, and Billie followed close behind me. The halls were dark. Barely enough light leaked through the windows to prevent us from bumping into corners. I wished I had thought to bring one of the lamps. I wished I had thought to bring the gun, too. It was still in the kitchen, on the drainboard. The pounding continued. It echoed curiously along the halls, repeating itself over and over, loud, then a few yards from the huge front door. The pounding had stopped, abruptly. I had the strange sensation that it had never happened, that we had imagined the noise.

'You're not going to *open* that door, are you?' Billie whispered, her voice hoarse.

'I don't know—'

'I wouldn't,' she said firmly.

We stood staring at the door, Billie's hand

gripping my own. Although the pounding had ceased, I could sense a presence behind the door. It was an acute sensation. I could feel someone standing, waiting, listening. I could almost hear a panting noise, but I knew that must be my imagination. There was another sound, almost like a whimper, and that was all too real. I felt cold chills crawling over my skin. Billie gripped my hand so tightly that I thought my fingers would break. I pulled my hand free and stepped towards the door.

'Em!' Billie protested. 'I think it would be best not to—'

My hand was already on the knob. I turned it and pulled the door open. A great gust of cold wind came rushing in, striking me in the face, fluttering my hair. The front porch was dense with shadow. Rain dripped loudly from the eaves of the veranda. I saw no one. I stepped out on the porch. I knew that I must be standing almost exactly where Henrietta had stood on the night she was murdered. I braced myself. I forced myself to be calm. There was no one in sight.

'Em—' Billie was right behind me, as puzzled as I.

'Someone was here,' I said, 'but—'

A dark form stirred among the shadows on the step. Billie screamed. I seized her arm.

Black waves washed over me, and I saw an axe, blood, heard screams, saw a head roll, all in a split second, and then a little boy stood in front of us, his face pale and worried, his shoulders trembling in the cold air. It was Sean Murphy.

'I didn't think anyone was at home,' he said in a thin voice. 'I had to sit down and rest a minute before I started back.'

'Sean—' I cried. 'You—you frightened us.'

'I'm sorry, Miss Rogers. I was just—is Betty here? Please tell her to come on out and come home. My mother is worried, you see, and Betty shouldn't do these things. Not when— please tell her to come on out, Miss Rogers.'

'But, Sean—'

'Please,' he said, his thin voice full of anguish. 'She's got to be here. Tell her—tell her she won't be punished. Just to come home. That's all. Mother's so worried, you see, and— and Betty's never been gone this long before and I've looked everywhere else, up and down and all her usual places and she wasn't at any of them so she's got to be here. Won't you get her for me?'

He stood there bravely, his arms at his sides, his hands clenched into tight little fists. He looked like a miniature adult with his well developed body and his solemn, sober face, but the corners of his lips quivered and his large brown eyes betrayed a child's fear. I could see that he wanted to break down and cry, but that would not have been manly. He stood with his shoulders thrown back, his jaw thrust out, and his eyes pleaded with me to say the words he wanted to hear.

Billie and I exchanged glances. She gnawed her lower lip.

'She isn't here, Sean,' I said quietly. 'She hasn't been here.'

'I was afraid of that,' he replied. His voice held firm.

'How long have you been looking for her?'

'For hours. She disappeared shortly after you left the store. At first we thought she'd just run off, but then—then she didn't come back. I knew something was wrong. Mother did too. I said I'd find her.'

'Maybe she's returned home while you were out looking,' I suggested. I could see the words were little comfort to him.

'Have you had dinner?' Billie asked. 'You haven't, have you? There's some stew left, and cheese. You come with me. You'll feel better after you eat something.'

'I couldn't eat,' he said simply. 'Thank you.'

'We'll drive you back to the store,' I said. 'Maybe Betty will be back when we get there.

If—if she isn't, we'll help you look for her. I'll go get the car and bring it around the front. You stay with Miss Mead. Billie, get the— uh—you know what. In the kitchen, on the drainboard. Put it in your purse.' I kept my voice deliberately light and airy. 'We might need it, I think.'

'Yes,' she replied blithely. 'We just might. Come on, Sean. You're wet. You'll catch a nasty cold. I'll get you a towel. You can dry off. Em, dear, are you going to the garage by yourself?'

'I'll have to,' I said.

'Luck,' she retorted.

'The keys are in the ignition, aren't they?'

'Should be. I'll bring your purse out.'

She put her arm around Sean's shoulder and led him inside. I went down the steps and started around the side of the house. The ground was wet and muddy. The air was fresh and cold. The moon was behind a bank of clouds, gilding them with silvery radiance, and the rest of the sky was light grey, wet. Everything was sharply etched, black against grey, and I could see clearly. The carriage house reared up at the end of the drive, swathed in shadows. The door yawned open, a great black hole with the rear fender of Clive's car projecting out of the darkness. There was no sign of Boyd. I walked towards the door. My shoes crunched noisily on the drive. I knew I couldn't step into that darkness. I knew I didn't have that kind of courage.

I pushed all thoughts out of my mind and stepped through the door.

It was pitch black. I could smell gasoline fumes and rusted metal. Someone was standing in the dark corner watching every move I made. In a moment he would leap out at me. I opened the car door and got behind the wheel. I fumbled on the dash and jerked the light switch. The headlights flooded the place with sharp yellow light. There was no one in the corner. Now he was sitting in the back seat of the car, raising his hand to lay it on my shoulder. I turned on the interior light. A pile of magazines and a scarf were on the back seat, nothing else. I backed the car out, turned it around in the space provided in front of the carriage house and drove around front. Billie and Sean came out a few minutes later.

'Did you get that certain item?' I asked Billie as we drove away.

'Mmm,' she nodded. 'Not on the drainboard, though. You left it on the high stool beside the stove. I looked and looked.'

'Did I? I could have sworn—oh well, you got it.'

'I put it in your purse. Has our friend left?'

'Apparently. The apartment was dark. There were no signs of anyone.'

I drove along the road Boyd had taken this afternoon. It was still wet, slippery now. I had to drive slower than I would have preferred. The headlights glistened on the wet pavement and made bright yellow sweeps over tree trunks and shrubs as I turned. Sean sat in front between us, his face grim. Billie had given him a towel to dry off with and replaced his wet shirt with a bulky navy blue turtle neck sweater which fit him remarkably well. She had also given him some crackers and cheese, and he ate them apologetically as we drove.

I found the turnoff and coasted down the road that led to the beach. I turned and started towards the shore. The sea was a sullen silver grey mass, hissing on the sand. The tacky little resort area looked shabbier than ever in the moonlight. The tiers of summer homes might house ghosts. The casino was a ruin washed with shadow. The whole place seemed desolate and deserted until we reached the store. It was ablaze with light. Three cars were parked in front of it, one of them a police car.

A policeman stood at the front door, barring our way. He wore a short, slick cape and a helmet with leather band fastened under his square jaw. He had a broken nose and dark, ugly eyes, and he scowled at us, his massive shoulders filling the doorway. Sean told him who we were, and he permitted us to move past him, blocking the doorway again as soon as we were inside. The store was brightly lighted, stark white light pouring down on colourful cartons and canned goods. A cluster of men stood around the counter, smoke from their cigars and cigarettes clouding the air.

Three of them wore police uniforms, and they stood around with their faces flushed and ruddy, their eyes grim. A fourth man wore a soiled blue suit and a grey and black tie hastily knotted. His thin brown hair was rumpled, and his pale, fleshy face looked sleepy. Despite all this, he had an air of authority that could never be mistaken. He saw us. He said something to one of the policemen and then hurried towards us. He held out his hand and I took it. I introduced Billie to Officer Stevens of the Brighton police.

'Miss Rogers, Miss Mead,' he said tersely. 'I was going to send for you. You've saved me the trouble.'

'Did Betty come back?' Sean asked, his eyes large and frightened.

'No, son, not yet,' Officer Stevens said, putting his hand on the boy's shoulder. 'You're back, though. That's one problem solved. You were gone for a long time. Your mother called us. She thought maybe you'd disappeared, too.'

'You wanted to see us?' I inquired.

'I thought maybe you knew something about the missing child. Evidently you don't.'

'I saw her this morning and again this afternoon when I came to buy my groceries.'

'Mother—' Sean began.

'She's all right, son. She's in her room. Why don't you go see her? She'll want you.'

Sean moved quickly to the door that led to the living quarters. I saw George Reed leaning against a wall of boxed cereals. His face was grave, the brown eyes dark with worry, deep creases in his cheeks. He was wearing the same clothes he had worn this afternoon, the white shirt with sleeves rolled up, the soiled white jeans and scuffed tennis shoes. He looked like a Greek statue suddenly endowed with life and bewildered by the odd clothes and strange surroundings.

'What's he doing here?' I asked. Officer Stevens glanced at Reed.

'We picked Reed up, brought him here,' he informed me. 'He was apparently the last one to see the child. He was on the pier down the beach a ways, talking to her. Around two-thirty or three this afternoon. Several people saw them together. He claims he left her there and went back to his cottage.'

'She's been missing that long?' I asked.

'I'm afraid so. We've got a search party out looking for her. It seems she runs away quite a lot, but she's never been gone this long. The widow called us a couple of hours ago. She'd sent the son out to find Betty, and when he didn't come back she finally phoned us.'

'It's terrible,' Billie whispered.

'That it is,' Officer Stevens said grimly. 'Missing child—suspicion of foul play—'

'You suspect foul play?' Billie asked in a faint voice.

'The mother does. Wouldn't tell us anything. Sat there like she was in a trance, just kept saying "He got her. He got her" over and over again. Shock, of course. She'll talk later on.' His sharp blue eyes looked into mine. He nodded slightly. 'I think this might have something to do with the other,' he said quietly.

'I'm sure it does,' I replied. My voice was shaky.

'It looks bad, Miss Rogers.'

'She knew something, it would seem.'

'She did. Betty saw something that night. She told me. She wouldn't give me any details, but she saw something. Someone found out.

Someone was afraid she—'

'Let's keep calm,' he said sternly. 'That's the only way.'

'The widow knows,' I said abruptly. 'Betty told her mother what she saw and her mother told her to keep quiet about it. She was frightened. She warned Betty not to say a word—but she did. She hinted around with me this morning, and—' I suddenly remembered seeing Betty with Gordon. I remembered her showing him the wooden animal Burt Reed had carved for her. I could feel the colour leaving my face.

'What is it?' Officer Stevens demanded brusquely.

'I—I think she told someone else,' I said in a voice that was barely audible.

'Who?'

'Gordon Stuart.'

'The brother?'

'Yes. He—he seemed very interested in whatever she was saying. They were talking together early this afternoon, while I was here doing my shopping.'

Officer Stevens nodded his head, his lids narrowed. He signalled one of his men to come over. He took the man aside and said something to him. The man made a telephone call behind the counter and then left the store. I stood beside Billie, gripping her hand tightly.

I closed my eyes for a moment. I took a deep breath. I forced back all the horrible visions that threatened to take root in my mind. I had to keep calm. I felt that I was partly to blame for all this, and I had to do something. I had to help.

'I want to see the widow,' I told Officer Stevens. 'She—she needs a woman right now. Perhaps she'll talk to me.'

'I doubt it,' he retorted. 'She's in a pretty bad state.'

'Let me try,' I insisted. 'It's important—'

'The boy needs something to eat,' Billie added firmly. 'I doubt if his mother is in any condition to see to it. He was out in the rain, and he needs to get out of those wet trousers and socks. There are probably a dozen things—'

'Go ahead,' Officer Stevens said. 'Both of you. You might be able to get something out of her. But—Emmalynn—uh, Miss Rogers—be careful. Be gentle. She's in shock, you know. Her little girl is missing. Be sure you don't say anything that would—'

'I think I can handle it,' I said crisply.

'I'm sure you can.' He stepped aside to let us pass.

We walked towards the door in the rear of the store. We had to pass in front of George Reed. He stood up straight to let us by. His eyes spoke to me, pleaded with me. He made as though to reach out and touch my arm. I gave him a frosty stare and moved on by. He sighed and leaned back against the wall of boxed cereals.

Widow Murphy was sitting on a shabby blue sofa in a tiny living room with faded violet paper on the walls and limp white curtains at the window. Her hands were folded primly in her lap, and her eyes stared without seeing. Tragedy had stamped her face. There were dark smudges under her eyes. Her thin lips were pale, twitching slightly at one corner. Sean sat beside her, looking helpless and utterly crestfallen. He looked up when we came in. Hope danced in his eyes for a brief instant, then vanished. He introduced us to his mother. She gave no response.

'Please, Mother, Miss Rogers and Miss Mead. Miss Mead let me wear this sweater. She gave me crackers and cheese. They want to help.'

'No one can help,' she said. She might have been talking in her sleep. 'He got her. I know he did.'

Billie and I exchanged glances. Billie frowned. She stepped over to the door that led to the kitchen and looked inside. The kitchen was small, cluttered with unwashed dishes. It smelled of grease. Billie pushed up her elbow length puffed sleeves and looked very resolute. She took Sean by the hand and led him towards the kitchen.

'We're going to wash these dishes and clean this place up,' she told him, 'and then we're going to make a nice hot meal. The two of us. First you're going to go to your room and take a hot, hot bath and put on pyjamas and robe. House shoes, too. While you're doing that I'll make coffee. Does your mother drink coffee?'

'Sometimes. The pot's in that cabinet.'

'I'll find everything for myself. You run on. Hustle, kid. I'm going to need plenty of help around here, and you're elected.'

I sat down beside Widow Murphy. I didn't say anything. I knew what she was going through, and I knew that words would be useless at the moment. I was relieved when Billie came in with two cups of coffee on a tray. She put the tray down on the small table in front of the sofa and went back to the kitchen. Widow Murphy took a cup of the steaming beverage and held it, her hands wrapped around it as though for warmth. I heard Billie splashing water in the sink, rattling pans. The domestic noises were comforting. The widow finally sipped her coffee. She set the cup down and turned to me.

'Sean—' she said. 'Wet clothes—'

'We're seeing to that. He's taking a hot bath right now. We're going to see that he gets a hot meal, too. I wish you'd eat something as well. I know you don't feel like it, but it'd be good for you.'

'You're kind, Miss Rogers. You always were.'

'You don't have to talk, Mrs Murphy. It isn't necessary. But if you would like to—'

'One must go on,' she said slowly. 'The blows come. One goes on. I have to think of that.'

'They'll find her, Mrs Murphy. You must believe that.'

Widow Murphy made no reply. She finished her coffee. It seemed to revive her somewhat. Her lips were not as white as before, and her eyes had lost that distant look. She glanced up when Sean came through the room. He was wearing a pair of long white pyjamas and a brown corduroy bathrobe. His skin glowed rosy from the bath and his hair was wet. His mother nodded. She watched him go into the kitchen.

'I have to tell someone,' she said haltingly. 'I may as well tell you. It's too late for it to matter now—now that Betty's gone. It will help the police bring justice. Justice didn't matter before. Now it does. Now my Betty is gone—'

'Mrs Murphy—'

'Let me talk. You were there that night, Miss Rogers. They say you saw. You understand what I'm talking about?'

'Of course,' I replied quietly.

'They say you saw and don't remember. I can understand that. It must have been a terrible shock—too terrible to keep in your mind. Betty saw something that night, too.'

She paused. She closed her eyes for a moment. I could hear something sizzling in the kitchen, and I smelled bacon. Sean was cracking eggs and plopping them into a large bowl. The normal noises coming from the kitchen made a chilling contrast with the tension and terror felt here in the living room.

'She used to run off all the time,' the widow continued. 'I couldn't do anything with her. She'd run off from school and prowl around. Everyone around here liked her. They were used to seeing her hanging about. She was a nosy child. She knew everything that went on. She even made notes about what she saw. That was bad enough. Then she started sneaking out of bed at night and going for long walks along the beach. I tried to put a stop to it. I tried everything—'

She sighed heavily and ran her hand over

the faded blonde hair pulled so tightly over her skull. She looked utterly exhausted, as though it had drained her energy to say this much. I thought for a while that she was going to slip back into the near-catatonic trance, but she pulled her back up rigid and folded her hands in her lap. She examined the hands as though she had never seen them before and wondered what such alien objects were doing in her lap. When she finally spoke again her voice was flat.

'I spanked her. She rebelled. I locked her in her room. She climbed out her window. Every other night she would go for a walk. Sometimes she'd be gone for fifteen minutes, sometimes an hour. The counsellor at school said it wasn't anything to be worried about. He used a lot of big words I couldn't understand and a lot of technical terms, but what he meant was she was growing up too fast and needed an outlet for her energy. He said not to worry, but I worried just the same.'

She pressed her lips tightly together. 'That night she was gone a long time, over an hour. She walked all the way to Burt Reed's cottage. He was her special friend. His light was on and he was sitting in his room making fishing lures. She was fascinated. She watched him twist the wires with a few coloured feathers and insert the hook. She said she thought she heard a scream, but it was so far away she didn't pay any attention to it. Then, a few minutes later, a man came towards the cottage. He had an axe—'

CHAPTER THIRTEEN

Her voice broke. A tear slid down her cheek. She wiped it away. Her shoulders quivered once, and she almost lost control. The hysteria that was inside threatened to break loose. The widow gripped the edge of the sofa and took a deep breath. She composed herself. It took great effort. Her dark brown eyes grew expressionless once again, and when she continued to speak her voice was toneless. 'She scrambled under a clump of bushes. The man began to thrash around in the bushes, looking for a good place to hide the axe. Once he touched her but it was dark and he didn't realize what he'd touched. He finally shoved the axe under a thick clump of bushes and left. Betty was petrified. It was ten minutes before she could move. She ran all the way home.'

My flesh seemed to have turned cold. I knew

my face wore an expression of pure horror. I could see the child cowering under the bushes, trembling as the man thrashed around her, coming closer, breathing heavily. I could feel her terror as his hand reached down, touched her. She must have wanted to scream, but she was frightened numb, her vocal cords paralysed. It was too horrible to contemplate. I chewed my lower lip and tried to force that picture out of my mind.

'Did she recognize the man?' I asked, trying to keep my voice level.

'No. It was too dark. He was big. That's all she could tell me. When he touched her she saw his hand. He was wearing gloves. That's all.'

I remembered the theory Billie had expounded this afternoon. The axe would naturally have Burt Reed's fingerprints on it, as he was the only one who would have handled it before it was stolen. The killer wore gloves each time he handled the axe, and, after he had murdered with it and hidden it, it would still have had only Reed's prints on it. It was almost too simple and, because of this same simplicity, devilishly clever.

'I was waiting for her when she came home,' the widow continued. 'She looked pale and scared, but she didn't say anything. I didn't press her. I could see she was upset, but I assumed it was because she was afraid of a spanking.'

'Did she tell you in the morning?'

Widow Murphy shook her head. 'She was silent and sullen all the next day, wouldn't speak to anyone. We heard the news over the radio. Then we heard that Burt Reed had been arrested. Betty came to me then. She told me everything. She was terrified. I was, too, but I knew we had to tell the police about it. I was afraid he would—would come after Betty, thinking she might identify him, but I knew I couldn't let that innocent man go to prison. I waited, thinking I'd have enough courage in a day or so to tell the police, and then Burt Reed died of a heart attack in his cell and there wasn't any reason to talk.'

'A murderer was loose,' I said.

'I couldn't afford to think of that.'

'If you had, Betty might be here today,' I said quietly.

'I couldn't do that,' she said. 'The risk—'

'I understand, Mrs Murphy. You were a mother.'

'I was wrong. I know that. I should have gone to the police immediately. I would have— to save Burt Reed. But when he died I could only think of my little girl. As long as no one knew, she was in no danger. I told her to keep quiet about it. I warned her of what might happen if she talked about it to anyone, and she understood. But time passed—' She stared down at her hands. 'Time passed, and nothing happened. The threat vanished and it was like something that had never happened. She wanted attention, and she found she could get it by bragging about her friendship with Burt Reed. She began to drop little hints here and there. She bragged to her schoolmates. I warned her. God knows I warned her.'

'Mrs Murphy—' I said hesitantly. 'Do you have any idea who might have done it?'

'The man,' she said. 'The son. He was talking to my baby this afternoon. People saw them together.'

'George Reed? You think he might have murdered Henrietta? But—why would he want to throw suspicion on his own father? Why would he spend all this time trying to prove his father was innocent?'

'I don't know anything about any of that,' she said in the same toneless voice. 'But I know he was always asking questions, always lurking around. My little girl was afraid of him. He's big. That man was big. He's one of these radicals—stirring up trouble all the time—and he was plenty mad when Mrs Stern made his father stop building.'

'It doesn't seem logical,' I protested.

Widow Murphy looked at me with those expressionless brown eyes. There was a bitter smile on her thin lips. 'Is any of this logical?' she asked. The lips trembled and the smile vanished. She sank back against the sofa, all energy and emotion depleted. No one could reach her now, not for a long time. I wanted to take her hand and pat it, but I knew that the gesture would have been futile. I doubted if she would even have been aware of this. I stood up, feeling completely helpless.

Billie was standing in the doorway to the kitchen, an apron tied over the jade green dress, her hair spilling over her shoulders.

'You heard?' I said quietly.

Billie nodded. 'What are you going to do?'

'I'm going to tell Officer Stevens everything she told me,' I replied. 'Then—I don't know what I'll do. I can't just sit around.'

'Em, don't do anything rash.'

'I can't just wait. I'll go to pieces.'

'I doubt that,' she said.

She glanced over her shoulder at Sean. He was sitting at the table, a piece of toast in his hand.

'I'm going to have a cup of that coffee,' Billie said, 'and then I'm going to see that he finishes his dinner and put him to bed. After that, I think I'll try to get her to eat something. She's in a bad way now, but in a little while she's going to need someone.'

Billie spoke in a quiet, sensible voice. She was completely in command of the situation. I wasn't at all surprised. The mod clothes and flippant mannerisms were deceiving only to people who didn't know what genuine character was made of. In a crisis, I'd take Billie anytime.

Officer Stevens was on the telephone when I returned to the front part of the store. The cigarette smoke was thicker than ever. The burly policemen looked even more ill at ease, more flushed. George Reed was gone. He had not been under any form of arrest. They had merely wanted to question him. Officer Stevens put down the phone and grimaced, his eyes narrowed, deep lines about his mouth. I asked him to step outside with me. We stood in the tiny parking lot beside the store. Clouds rolled over the moon, but there was still enough light for me to see his face as I told him everything the widow had said.

'So Reed was innocent,' he said grimly. 'The proof was there all along and we had no way of knowing. If only the woman had talked. It would have saved a great deal of trouble.' He shook his head, his hands in the pockets of the wrinkled blue suit. A gust of wind fluttered his tie up against his shoulder.

'A little girl is missing,' I said. 'That's the only important thing right now.'

'We'll find her. And we'll get him.'

'I'm sure of it,' I told him. 'My memory is coming back—quickly. I'm remembering more and more—'

'You think you can tell me who the killer is?'

'By morning,' I said.

'I don't like this, Emmalynn. I feel responsible for you. You're in a dangerous position.'

'No more so than I have been in up 'til now.'

'I think we'd better pack up and send you back to London. We can't run the risk of—'

'Just concentrate on finding that child,' I retorted.

One of the policemen came out to tell Officer Stevens that he had received another telephone call. Stevens left, his shoulders stooped, his face lined. I walked around the store and stood on the pier where Gordon and I had talked this afternoon. I rested my hands on the wooden railing. I could hear the water swirling beneath the wooden planks. The sea was inky black. Far out a ship flashed red and white signals, mere pinpoints of light. The moon came out from behind the clouds. Everything was washed in a murky silver glow.

I tried to relax. I tried to make my mind a blank. It was useless. I kept thinking about Betty Murphy with her pixie face and shaggy blonde hair and cocky, audacious mannerisms. It was a dark night, and cold. She was out there somewhere. I squared my shoulders and went quickly to the car. I knew there was a flashlight in the glove compartment. I got it. I knew I had no business doing what I was about to do, but I couldn't help myself. I couldn't just sit and wait and watch the clock and pray and hope. I had to act.

I moved beyond the lights of the store and disappeared into the darkness. I couldn't use the flashlight yet. They would try to stop me if they saw me leaving. A whole search party was out looking for Betty, and it was preposterous to think I might find her where they failed, but at least I would be moving, at least I would be doing something. Fifty yards from the store a flight of rickety wooden stairs twisted and turned down a shelf of rock and led to the beach below. I moved down them cautiously, holding on to the railing. The stairs were hazardous, the wood near-rotten. I could feel each step give way a little as I put my weight on it. There was just enough moonlight for me to see how to get down without hurtling forward over the jagged rocks that projected up all around the stairs.

As I moved down I remembered the gun. It was in my purse. I had left the purse with Billie. I frowned. I didn't really need the gun. It would have been nice to have with me just the same. I went on down the stairs.

Below there was nothing but sand and rock and sea. The smooth, cultivated expanse of beach where children played and bathers lolled was further on down the shore line. Here the waves were angry, the rocks treacherous, the sand gritty and littered with shells. The thundering noise of the water as it hurled itself against the rocks was deafening. Salty spray stung my cheeks. I felt I had stepped into the middle of a nightmare with the chaos of noise and the tormented shadows that danced about the rocks. I switched on the flashlight. The thin yellow spear of light only heightened the dark around me.

I swerved the flashlight left and right. The yellow ray slid over the sand, brushed over the wet grey faces of rock, picked out pieces of driftwood in my path. There was perhaps twenty yards of beach between the waterline and the shelf of rock that reared up, but it widened as I moved further away from the resort areas. Soon the shelf of rock was gone and I was on an expanse of beach much like that where Betty had shown me the dog Burt Reed had carved for her. The large rocks no longer projected out of the water. Here the beach was smooth. The waves washed over the shingles with a sucking sound. The sand was wet under my feet. Large pieces of driftwood littered the beach, and to one side of me the sand dunes began to rise up in grassy humps.

The moonlight was pale with a greenish glow. Mist swirled in the air in thin tendrils broken and torn by the wind. I almost stumbled over an old deserted rowboat with its sides caved in, barnacles clinging to the rotten wood. Now that the moon was out from behind the clouds I really had no need for the flashlight. I switched it off. I might need it later, and it was best to preserve the batteries. I moved slowly along the beach in the direction of the Stern place, taking the route I knew Betty must have taken this morning.

I had no real hopes of finding her, but I studied every foot of the way, and I called her name, over and over again. The search party must have already covered this area, for I saw no signs of them. They were probably further inland now, going through the woods with their lanterns and short wave radios. I thought I heard voices calling far away, but it might have been the wind swishing through the tall brown grass or a seagull confused by the night.

Betty is merely lost, I told myself. How could she be lost? She must know this area backwards and forwards. She fell and hurt herself. Yes, she fell. She's waiting, patiently waiting, knowing we'll find her. She's all alone. Frightened. They must find her. I must find her.

These thoughts darted over the surface of my mind like frantic birds, fighting furiously to keep back the dreaded fear that threatened to blot everything else out. I couldn't allow myself to think of the more logical explanation for her disappearance. If I let that thought take root, I would be utterly defeated.

The heel of my shoe caught on the edge of a rock. I pitched forward and landed on my hands and knees. I climbed back up on weakened legs. It must have been thirty minutes since I left the store. I was out of breath. My throat was hoarse from calling Betty. The air was damp with sea, and it was getting colder by the minute. I stood very still, my hands pressed to my temples. I could feel the pulses throbbing. I stumbled on, and it was several minutes before I realized I had dropped the flashlight when I had fallen down. I was too tired to go back for it. There was plenty of moonlight. I wouldn't need the flashlight.

The moon was promptly veiled with clouds. The greenish-white expanse of sand turned blue-black. The clouds drifted away, and the beach gleamed again, became a floor of shifting shadows as more clouds were blown across the surface of the moon. I stopped. I listened. I thought I heard someone calling my name. It sounded like a hoarse whisper from this distance. Emmalynn...the word echoed in the air and then evaporated, and it was not repeated. I must have imagined it. Who could have been calling me? I felt an icy chill inside. I had to force myself to move on.

I saw a small wooden pier stretching out over the water ahead. It was a mere ruin, beginning a few feet from the water's edge and ending not ten yards further out. Some of the planks had broken in two and hung down like jagged fingers that reached for the water. There was a tiny hut, too, one side collapsed, the rest leaning precariously. There was something ghostly about the scene, bathed in the silver-green glow of moonlight and partially veiled by the tendrils of mist that swirled like lost souls. I wondered if some fisherman had once lived here. A circle of rocks in front of the hut contained wet ashes and lumps of charcoal. It all looked as bizarre and mysterious as some Druid encampment deserted centuries ago.

I stepped over to the hut. Rays of shimmering moonlight poured through the remnants of the roof to reveal an earthen floor littered with rubbish. Motes of dust swirled in the rays of light, and a horrible fetid odour rose from a pile of rags heaped in one corner. I started to turn away. Something held me there. For a moment I did not know what it was. Something had registered. Something had caught my eye...I saw a broken porcelain pot, a rusty frying pan, half a dozen cans, and there, touched by a ray of light and bathed in silver, the tiny wooden dog Betty had shown me this morning. I picked it up, held it in the palm of my hand, stared at it in horror. I could feel my whole body trembling.

Betty treasured this carving. It was her prize possession. She kept it snug in the pockets of her jeans, taking it out only to show to people she trusted. She had shown it to me. She had shown it to Gordon Stuart. Who else had she shown it to? What was it doing on the floor of this forsaken hut? There had to be some reason. The water rushed over the shingles with that monotonous sucking sound. Filmy sheets of mist broke and fragmented. The cold wind blew through the stiff brown grass and caused it to crackle. I stared at the tiny wooden dog in the palm of my hand as though it were an object endowed with magic powers.

The noises of the beach stirred around me, the wind, the waves. The poles of the old pier creaked. Somewhere a cricket rasped noisily. I was not aware of the new sound at first. It blended with the others, camouflaged by them. I dropped the carving into my pocket and stared out at the inky black water that swelled and churned and came rushing over the sand. I seemed to be paralysed. The cold wind chilled my skin and whipped my hair. Made immobile by the night and my own fear, I closed my eyes, shutting out everything, and seconds passed. It was then that I heard the new sound. I could not identify it at first. It was a pounding, crunching noise, coming towards me from the part of the beach I had already covered. I listened with my brows pressed together, trying to place the sound. Footsteps, running towards me....

'Emmalynn—'

The wind caught the word and shattered it. It was a hoarse cry. I did not recognize the voice. I peered down the beach. Through the shadows and the floating tendrils of mist I could barely see the man. He was far away, a dark form coming closer. He shouted again but the roar of the sea drowned his voice. I watched him coming towards me, my body stiff, my blood cold. It was a nightmare. It wasn't real. I wondered vaguely who he was and what he wanted with me. You'll wake up, I told myself, and it will all be over. My fear was so strong I was numb from it, held captive in its grip. He was coming closer. I could hear him panting now. I tried to scream. No sound would come.

I don't know how long I stood watching with horrified eyes. It seemed an hour. It couldn't have been more than a few seconds. The panic broke. My body moved instinctively. I looked towards the hut. No refuge there. I saw the waves swelling up and spilling over the shingles. Cut off. I had no hope of outrunning him. I ran towards the sand dunes, stumbled around one of the great humps, fell, got to my feet, moved around another and another until I was surrounded by mounds of earth overgrown with stiff brown grass. The clouds blew across the surface of the sky. The moon was completely exposed, a misshapen round ball that gilded the area with unwanted light. The glass rustled all around me with a fierce, threatening sound.

I moved on and on, my heart pounding, my lungs threatening to burst. I was lost in the forest of sand dunes, some of them rising up over my head and others mere lumps of earth waist high. I ran away from the sound of the sea. I turned. I was going back towards the beach. I paused, confused, my sense of direction shattered by the panic. I heard him. He was moving noisily towards me, but the noise swelled and echoed and I could not tell which way it was coming from. I heard feet crunching on sand. I heard panting. I heard a splintering crash as he stepped on a bit of driftwood. The noises came from all sides, now near, now far. They ceased. There was a second of silence underlined by the wash of sea over shingles, a sound much like laboured breathing.

'Emmalynn. I want you.'

The voice was hoarse. I thought I recognized it, but I could not be sure.

'Don't run, Emmalynn. It's me—'

I stood very still in the shadows of a towering sand dune. I took off my shoes. I removed my stockings. I made as little noise as possible. The sand was cold and gritty to my bare feet, but I found I could move without noise. That was a definite advantage. I crept around the dune. In front of me was a small clearing, the sand silver bright. I darted across it. I knew he must have seen me. I could hear him thundering after me. I circled around the clearing, winding behind huge humps, and finally I could go no longer. My heart felt as though it were about to explode.

I dropped to the ground in the shadows of a dune, behind a large piece of driftwood. I crouched against the earth, breathing rapidly, peering out through a branch of the wood. I knew it would be practically impossible for him to see me. I heard him quite near. He stumbled against a mound, slid down, cursed. He couldn't be ten yards away. The moonlight streamed down, gilding the tops of the dunes with a silvery green glow and providing dense shadows below. The sea sounded far away, sounded more than ever like heavy breathing. I managed to catch my breath, control it, breathe evenly and quietly. He stepped around a dune.

He was silhouetted against the moonlight, black against silver. I saw only the tall dark shape and the grotesque shadow that loomed away from it, moving when he moved. He stood there only an instant. He smashed his fist in the palm of his hand. He cursed again, a gutteral noise deep in his throat. He moved away. I could hear his footsteps plodding on the ground. He moved off in another direction, away from me. He called my name again. I lay flat on the ground, my lower lip between my teeth. Finally there was no noise but the wind in the grass and the scratching sound made by a small sand creature disturbed by all this activity in his domain.

Five minutes passed, ten, perhaps more. My whole body felt numb. I was freezing there on the damp earth. I stood up cautiously. I couldn't be sure he was gone. Perhaps he was resting, too. Perhaps he was waiting for me to come out of hiding. I listened. There were no disturbing noises. I walked slowly around the sand dune and began moving away from the sea. If I went back to the beach, he would see me. Here, at least, there were shadows to help conceal my progress. The sand dunes began to thin out, spread further and further apart. The land sloped down. I walked across a field, tall grass waving knee-high. There was a small ravine, and beyond it dark woods. Fireflies played in the woods, tiny points of yellow light darting here and there among the trees.

I stepped to the edge of the ravine. The ground sloped down gently for perhaps ten feet to where a dry river bed twisted and turned. On the other side there were two or three acres of grassy field, and then the woods began. The woods seemed to be full of activity. I heard a buzzing sound. I suddenly realized that the darting lights were not fireflies at all. They were lanterns, seen from afar. The buzzing sound was made by many voices, muffled by the thickness of trees and shrubs. It must be the search party, I thought. I started down the ravine, my bare feet tormented by tiny rocks and bits of shell.

'Emmalynn—wait—'

The voice came from behind me. He was coming across the field towards me. I stumbled down the ravine, and I saw her. She was on her stomach, her head turned to one side, her arms spread out. I kneeled beside her. I lifted her cold little body in my arms, ran my hand over her face. She was breathing jerkily. There was a cut on the side of her face, and one arm did not hang right. Her eyes opened and she stared at me. Her lips moved. I bent my head down to catch the words.

'He tried to get me,' the child whispered hoarsely. 'I ran away. I hid—in the hut. He found me. He hit me—hard. He hurt my arm. I woke up. I ran—I ran. I fell down here—' And then the lips grew still and the eyes closed.

I called out, again and again. The lights in the woods began to move slowly towards the ravine. The buzzing sound increased, and I could make out individual words now: A woman. Over there. Beyond the field. In the ravine. What? The child. She's found her. I held Betty in my arms, her tiny body limp against mine. I stroked her hair. I prayed she would be all right.

Rocks slid down the slope of ground. I looked up. He was standing at the edge of the ravine, his hands on his hips, staring down at me. Across the ravine, men were breaking out of the woods and running over the field. I could hear their footsteps. George Reed came cautiously down the slope. His thick brown hair fell straight across one brow. His horn-rimmed glasses glittered. The lines of his Slavic face showed deep concern. He heaved his heavy shoulders and stood over me.

'You ran,' he said, his voice low. 'You ran from me.'

'She's alive,' I whispered. 'She's alive! That's all that matters.'

CHAPTER FOURTEEN

Billie and I were silent during the drive back to the house. It seemed ages had passed since Sean first knocked on the front door, but it was just now ten o'clock. So much had happened in such a short time. Betty was in the hospital now, under the care of a Doctor Martin. He had set her broken arm and given her sedatives and informed the police that it would be at least two days before she would be able to answer their questions. She hadn't regained consciousness after speaking to me, and we had no way of knowing who was responsible for her disappearance and subsequent injuries. Doctor Martin assured us that, with the exception of her arm being in a cast, Betty would soon be back to normal. I doubted seriously that she would mind the cast. She would be the proper little heroine among her school chums. The cast would merely add an extra element of glamour to that role, and all the attention she had longed for would be hers in abundance.

Widow Murphy was at the hospital, too, sitting at her daughter's bedside, where she would remain for the rest of the night. Neighbours had come to look after Sean, and there had been nothing left that Billie and I could do to help. Officer Stevens had not liked the idea of our going back to the house, but I had assured him that Doctor Clarkson would be there soon, if he wasn't there already, waiting for us.

The police had questioned George Reed thoroughly. He was able to explain his actions quite logically. He had been walking back to his cottage, he claimed, and he had seen me alone on the beach. He had wanted to speak to me. He called my name. I ran. He came after me, but he did not 'chase' me. I had to admit that I had run without knowing who was calling me, that he had called out several times identifying himself and that I hadn't recognized the voice. The police weren't entirely satisfied with Reed's story, but they had no way of disproving it. He had been vague and evasive when they asked what he wanted to speak to me about, merely telling them that it was 'a personal matter.' As we left the hospital I looked around for Reed, but he had evidently already gone back to his cottage. I wondered what that 'personal matter' was.

The tyres hummed over the road. The motor coughed and spluttered. The whole car shook as I turned down the poorly paved road that led through the dense wooded area and on to the house. The headlights glowed like two pale yellow spears through the mist that danced and swirled across the road. We circled out of the woods and could see the house ahead, a gaunt, forbidding relic, towering out of the mist. Dr Clarkson's car was not out front. I had hoped he would be waiting for us. I drove Clive's car into the garage and parked it. Neither Billie nor I said a word as we walked around the house and went inside. We had left an oil lamp burning in the front hall and its golden glow seemed to lick the dark walls and heighten the long shadows the ponderous furniture cast across the floor.

The house was silent and tomblike. All the rest of it was shrouded in darkness, and it seemed to be waiting for us. The doors in the hall opened into dark, dusty rooms thronging with shadows, and the staircase spiralled up like a live thing arrested in some act of evil. It was easy to imagine whispering voices and stealthy footsteps. I could tell Billie felt the way I did. Her face was pale, and there were dark smudges under her eyes. Her lips were turned down slightly at the corners, but her chin was resolute. I sighed deeply.

'Doctor Clarkson should be here soon,' I said.

'I know. I wish I were very, very brave.'

'We have the gun. It's here in my purse.'

'Small comfort,' she replied, striving for lightness. 'This really is madness, you know, Em.'

'It's almost over,' I assured her.

'Think so?'

I nodded. She rested her hands on her hips and shook her head.

'And to think I could have had a week in

Majorca, posing for *Punch*. I suppose this *is* more interesting, but in the future I intend to do a lot of reading about murder and stay miles away from the real thing. You look ghastly, Em. I suggest a hot bath. Under the circumstances, a bath will suffice, un-hot though it must be.'

She smiled, a brave smile. Both of us wanted to get far away from the house, but neither of us were going to give way to nerves. Billie would be Billie, blithe though shaken, and I would manage somehow to maintain at least a surface calm.

'I'm going to light lots of lamps and candles,' Billie told me, 'and while you're bathing I'll brew some tea. Doctor Clarkson will appreciate a cup when he gets here. That'll be right away. I hope.'

The bath was not a comfortable one. The old green marble tub was large and roomy, and the soap and water were wonderful. I squeezed the sponge and let streams of water pour over my shoulders, and I experienced a peculiarly sensual satisfaction as I lathered my legs with soapy foam, but all the while I kept listening for sinister footsteps. I kept glancing at the doorknob to see that it did not turn. A single oil lamp, perched on the edge of the sink, cast flickering black shadows over the dark green walls, the light reflecting weirdly in all the tarnished brass fixtures. I kept remembering that particularly gruesome scene in *Psycho,* and it was with some relief that I stepped out of the tub and wrapped myself with a gigantic white towel.

I put on a white turtle neck sweater and a short brown skirt, lavishly pleated. I slid my feet into a pair of brown sandals and sat down in front of the mirror to brush my hair. I brushed it vigorously, bringing out the deep copper highlights, and I found it a very soothing, normal occupation. Everything will go well, I told myself. Everything will go as planned. Doctor Clarkson will come—he may be downstairs already—and nothing will go wrong, as long as I remain calm. I put down the brush and stared at myself in the mirror. The eyes seemed too large, too dark, and the skin seemed to be stretched too tightly over the cheekbones, but there were no signs of hysteria. I was beginning to feel better. Bathing, dressing, brushing my hair: these simple, ordinary actions helped reestablish my equilibrium and drive the nervous fancies away.

I took an oil lamp and walked out into the darkness of the upper hall. It was cold. The wind coming through the opened windows whisked along the walls with a whispering sound, and the curtains billowed and grew limp and billowed again. The old floor groaned as I walked over it, but I did not hesitate. I started down the staircase. Halfway down there was a large rubber tree plant in a black pot. I almost dropped the lamp when one of the dead leaves brushed against my cheeks. Each step had its own peculiar sound, dull, shriek, creak, groan, and the noises echoed up in the well of silence. I ignored them all. No one was following me. No one was leaning over the railing above, watching me as I descended. I was rather pleased with my own calm as I stepped into the library.

Billie had lighted all the red glass lamps, and they glowed dimly from every part of the room, illuminating the walls of books, revealing the nest of shadows behind the overstuffed chair in one corner. Billie was curled up on the sofa a book in her lap, a curious expression on her face. A squat brown teapot set on the table in front of her, fragrant steam curling from the spout, and there was a platter of small cakes beside it. Billie sat up and put the book aside as I came in. There was a tiny crease on her brow, and her eyes looked dark and puzzled. I could tell that something was bothering her.

'Doctor Clarkson hasn't arrived yet?' I asked.

'Not yet,' she replied vaguely. 'Em—'
'Yes?'
'This book—'
'What is it?'
'The diary. Her diary. I came up and got it while you were bathing. I've just read it.'
'Already?'
'It isn't long. It's—going to surprise you, Em.'
'Will it?'
She nodded slowly. 'I—couldn't believe it at first. Too improbable! And then I read on—and there's no doubt.'
'What are you talking about?'
'You'll see. Em, I know who did it.'
'Who?'
'She doesn't call him by name, but it's perfectly clear. Oh, there's a letter too. Very puzzling. I was trying to figure it out when you came in.'
'A letter?'
'It was tucked between the pages of the book. It's very old, yellowing. Here. See if you can make anything of it.'
She handed me the letter. It was creased and soiled, crumbling at the edges. I sat down in the large chair and studied the letter in the glow of one of the lamps. It was dated 1938 and came from Devon. The handwriting was large and

scrawling, clearly that of an uneducated person, and the ink had faded to a dingy brown. I read it twice:

Mrs Stern,
We'll do just like you say, I'm sure, and no questions asked, but Herb and me are a bit worried if it's exactly proper. We're grateful to you, sure, as you've enabled us to experience a joy the Good Lord in his wisdom didn't see fit for us to know. The money you sent is a blessing. Herb will be able to make the farm a real farm now.
But is it honest? Sure we're grateful and understand your position and know why you want it this way and thank the Lord you didn't choose the solution that a great many fine ladies choose if I'm to believe the things I hear and read in the papers.
But is it fair to all concerned?
I don't intend to bother you any more, and the money was a blessing and you don't have to send any more unless you feel like it. I want you to know Herb and I don't intend to let on to anyone and you're in no danger that way, but I can't live a lie and I intend to be honest with those near and dear, already near and dear. That's best. Wishing you luck.
                              Enda Hodges

Billie had poured tea for both of us. I put the letter aside and took my cup. I sipped the tea, thinking about what I had just read. There was something about it that struck a responsive cord inside me, something that furnished an answer to a question that had been worrying me for quite some time, but it was all vague and confused in my mind, swimming near the surface but remaining just out of reach. At the moment I couldn't even think what it was the letter supplied an answer for.

'Does it mean anything to you?' Billie asked.

'I'm not sure. It seems to be telling me something. Something is ringing in the back of my mind, but I can't say just what it is.'

'The woman keeps mentioning money. It would seem Henrietta had given the Hodges a lot of money—enough to re-finance a farm, anyway. From what you've told me about her, I wouldn't imagine charity was one of Henrietta's strong points.'

'It wasn't. She was extremely tight.'

'Perhaps they had been blackmailing her. The woman says she didn't intend to "bother" her any more and that Henrietta didn't "have" to send more money.' Billie frowned, her head held a little to one side. 'I believe the letter is important, or why would she have saved it?

Why would it have been stuck between the pages of the book unless it had some connection?'

'I suppose I'd better read the diary—'

Billie threw up her hand, cutting me off. She was very still, listening. I listened, too, and I thought I heard a faint rumbling noise, then a muffled bang. The noises were both very quiet, more a matter of vibration than actual sound. Billie's face was pale, and I gripped the edge of the chair, waiting. I watched the ornate clock on the top of the mantel. The second hand moved slowly, jerkily. A minute passed, and it seemed more like ten. I watched the slender black hand traverse the face two more times and then heard Billie sigh. She stared at me with enormous eyes.

'Did I imagine that?' she asked.

'I don't know. It sounded like a car.'

'I thought so, too. I thought it might be Doctor Clarkson coming, but he'd have already knocked on the door by now.'

'We're both on edge,' I said. 'It was probably nothing.'

'Probably,' she replied, clearly not convinced.

'Let me see the diary,' I said.

She handed me the limp red volume and began to prowl around the room, examining titles of books in the dim light, touching things, moving restlessly from place to place. She was eager to discuss something with me and couldn't do it until I had studied the diary. I opened the book and began to read. The entries followed no orderly system. None of them were dated, and it was frequently difficult to tell if Henrietta were writing about the past or the present. Seeing that brisk, flamboyant handwriting disturbed me at first, for it was charged with the personality of the woman who had written it. It was almost as though Henrietta were talking to me. I could hear her crisp, cackling voice as I read.

The diary jumped and rambled. Henrietta wrote about her youth, about days long since gone, and she related insignificant bits of gossip concerning the people she saw day by day: the butcher, the mailman, the woman who came to collect alms for the needy. There was a humorous passage about her encounter with Betty, when she chased the child away from the window, and a full and rather salty account of her feud with Burt Reed. There were other entries, too, passages that caused me to feel first surprise and then a steadily mounting horror. I read without stopping.

I closed the book. I held it in my lap I sat very still. My eyes were dry, but they felt hot and seemed to sting. Billie watched me from across the room. She understood. She didn't say anything. After a while I opened the book again to reread certain entries that seemed to leap out from the pages of trivia and gossip. The first came near the front of the book, after a description of our arrival, and a series of complaints about the condition of the house:

He came today. Damn! Why must I be haunted? He won't leave. He wants money. They all want money. I told him it was all gone. He laughed at me. I've done my part. I don't want anything else to do with him. I don't care what he does as long as he leaves me alone. People say blood is thicker than water. I say hogwash. I might be unnatural, but I wouldn't care if he were dead. He's not well. There is something about him that frightens me. He's smooth on the surface, but underneath that I sense something dark and evil, evil....

I flipped over pages that detailed her dislike of medicines and my own persistence in bringing her pills and tonics. This was followed by another brief entry:

I had a bad spat with Emmalynn this morning. I treated her abominably. I really am an old terror! I wanted to apologize to her, but my pride prevented me. I ordered those new novels she wanted, though, and had the man at the swank shop sent out two cashmere sweaters. She's my only comfort, my only luxury. I intend to make it up to her, though she doesn't know it. He thinks he will get what's left. He's going to be surprised! I intend to keep an eagle eye on Emmalynn's inheritance. I'm going to fix it so he won't be able to touch it, no matter what he thinks he can prove in court....

There was a long swirling line and a blot of ink at the bottom of the page, as though she'd had to put the book away hastily. Someone must have walked in. I read the next entry:

He threatened me today. He says he needs money desperately. He wants to get out of the country. He wants to make a new start. I told him everything was gone. He knows about my reserve. Somehow he found out about it. I didn't think anyone knew, but he does, I'm sure. He must have seen them when I took them out of the drawer, that day I decided I needed a better hiding place. They were in my purse all day. He must have seen them....

I reread the entry. So Doctor Clarkson had

been wrong. The highly improbable was true after all. I was not really surprised. I had lived with Henrietta long enough to know that the improbable was precisely what to expect from her. I continued to read:

This morning Emmalynn went for a long walk. She thinks I don't know *why* she's so fond of fresh air. I have a pair of binoculars, and I've watched her talking to that man. He's no good for her. I'd like to tell her so. Maybe I will. While she was gone *he* came up to my room. Scared the life out of me. I turned around and there he was, standing in the doorway, smiling with his eyes flat and hard and hating. We had quite a quarrel. He said he'd kill me. I said I'm just an old woman who can't live very much longer anyway so go ahead, do it. He didn't say anything for a long time. His face was like a mask, all flat, no expression, and then suddenly he laughed with his eyes still hating and said he knew how he'd make me do what he wanted. He'd kill Emmalynn. He meant it. He couldn't kill me. It would be unnatural, and he'd never find what he's after, but he would kill her. He'd do it to hurt me. I've got to get her away from here. I can't tell her why. I can't tell anyone. I must make her leave, before he can carry out his threat....

I stared at the words, dancing blue swirls and loops that moved across the paper gaily. My eyes seemed to lose the ability to focus, and the words writhed and curled on the paper, ugly things, alive and evil. I waited for the sensation to pass and then turned to the last two entries:

She's gone at last. I've finally gotten rid of her. The girl has the patience of Job. I've been impossible for the past week, pushing her further and further. I would rant and rave and she'd stay calm and give me a pill or simply walk out of the room. I finally succeeded this morning. We had a violent argument over her secret romance, which never was a secret to me. I told her she wasn't to see him anymore. She went red in the face and said it was her life and she'd do what she wanted with it and I said oh no, not as long as she stayed in this house. She said she'd leave. I laughed and said she didn't have the guts. She packed her bags and left. Oh God, it hurt. I don't want her to hate me. I'm an old sinner, but I love that girl like she was my own....

I know what he would like to do, but he hasn't got the courage to do it. He's weak, not at all like me. Last night I heard him prowling around the house, searching. He crept down the hall and opened the door to my room and I was awake but didn't let on. He just stood there in the doorway, looking at me, and finally he went away and I heard him mumbling as he left. I'm not afraid of him. Now that Emmalynn's gone and I know he can't hurt her I have nothing to fear. He can lurk around, and he can threaten me all he likes, but I know he won't touch me. He couldn't. There are certain crimes that would be crimes against nature. So I'll wait, and he'll grow tired of his little game and go away. He must....

I understood so much now, and my grief was greater. It would be a part of me for a long time to come, but I had no time to examine it now. Now, I had to put it aside and summon forth a steel-like calm to carry me through. I closed the book and put it on a table and stood up. The room was cold. I folded my arms across my breast and looked at Billie. She was standing by the black marble hearth, her face pale in the shadows.

'It hurt?' she said quietly.
'A lot,' I replied.
'The diary explains everything.'
I nodded.

'It was Gordon Stuart,' she said.

'No,' I said. 'You've forgotten the letter.'

'But she said he—'

'Exactly. She said *he*. She never called him by name. She used a pronoun throughout the diary, although she readily identified everyone else. Don't you think that's curious?'

'I wondered.'

'It's basic psychology,' I said. 'She'd denied his existence for all these years, refused to give him a name. By using a pronoun instead of his name she was merely following a pattern she'd followed for years, refusing to recognize him.'

Billie frowned. She still didn't understand.

'The letter,' I said. 'There *was* a connection. A major one.'

I watched her face. It showed deep puzzlement, then surprise, then enlightenment. She looked at me with wide eyes, her lips parted, and then the eyes grew dark with fear.

'My God,' she whispered. 'All this time—'

'I know. It chills the blood.'

'We've got to get out of here, Em.'

'We're going to, just as soon as we get the jewels.'

'You know where they are?'

'Henrietta was quite clear about it.'

'I don't see—'

'Think.'

'She said—yes, of course: "I intend to keep an eagle eye on Emmalynn's inheritance—" '

'They're bound to be there,' I said.

I took the gun out of my purse. The metal was icy cold to the touch. I wrapped my fingers around it tightly and held it at my side. Billie took up one of the lamps and we left the room, Billie close behind me, the lamp casting red-gold shadows on the walls. We stood at the bottom of the staircase for a moment, both hesitant, both afraid. Cold air drifted down in chilly currents that felt clammy on our cheeks and arms. I gripped the gun even tighter. Billie took a deep breath. We started up into the shifting, stirring shadows of the stairwell.

CHAPTER FIFTEEN

I had left a light burning in my room. It was not burning now. Perhaps the cold breeze billowing through the opened windows had blown it out. The hall was washed with darkness, the walls coated black, and the lamp Billie held only underlined and emphasized this darkness. We paused at the top of the stairs. The breeze stopped blowing. The curtains fell limp. Everything grew still, quiet, but there was a sense of motion all around us, subtle and shifting. I had the curious sensation that the house was my enemy, that it had been holding back, gathering force, and now this stillness was the stillness before attack. Billie must have felt it too. She was breathing heavily, as though with difficulty, and the hand holding the lamp trembled visibly.

I led the way down the hall to Henrietta's old room. We went inside. I closed the door. Billie set the lamp down on a marble topped table, and we stared at each other in the flickering yellow glow. Billie tried a flippant smile to show me she wasn't really afraid, but the smile failed. Her eyes were dark, and her cheekbones looked chalky. I sighed and put the gun down beside the lamp. It was a moment before I could speak.

'It'll just take a moment,' I said.

'Hurry, Em.'

'I'll get something to stand on.'

The eagle perched on top of the tall, heavy wardrobe, out of reach. The yellow-green glass eyes seemed to be watching us in the wavering light. I moved a small velvet footstool to the edge of the wardrobe and climbed up on it, reaching for the eagle. I shivered as my fingers touched the dead, mouldy feathers. The eagle was heavy, far too heavy, and I lifted it down and set it on the table. It stared at us accusingly as it perched there on its black wooden pedestal. Billie backed away from it a little, as though she feared it would fly in her face.

'I've never seen anything so hideous,' she whispered.

'We'll have to find something to cut it open,' I replied.

'I don't think I could touch it.'

I stepped over to the old roll-topped desk and there, among the dusty coloured glass paperweights, I found a brass letter opener. The blade was dull, but it would do. I moved back to the table and stood over the eagle, wondering where I should make the first incision. The yellow-green eyes glared at me as though alive and aware of my intentions. I closed my eyes and plunged the knife into its chest. The eagle seemed to wince with pain. A cloud of dust exploded and feathers littered the table. I split the body open and reached inside, shuddering. I pulled out the worn chamois pouch. It was heavy and lumpy, tied with a piece of cord at the top. The eagle toppled over on the table, a limp pile of dust and feathers, destroyed.

We did not say anything. We stared at the bag. The excitement and elation we might have felt was overshadowed by the fear that hung like a tangible thing in the small, cluttered room with its sour smell and dust. We had no desire to examine the contents of the pouch. We wanted only to get away from this room, this house. I picked up the gun. Billie took the lamp and the lumpy chamois pouch. I touched the doorknob with trembling fingers. We heard the floor outside groan under the weight of something heavy moving across it.

I froze. Billie drew in her breath sharply.

The noise was repeated, a stealthy sound.

Strangely enough, the sound had a calming effect on both of us, like a bucket of cold water in the face of hysteria. The sound was real, something that we could hear and realize and therefore fight, whereas a moment before we had been in the grip of an unknown terror, a sinister pall that hung over us like a dark cloud. The knowledge of real danger is much less frightening than the silent threat of evil. My hand tightened on the doorknob. Billie held the lamp up. Her hand was steady.

'He's out there,' she whispered.

'I think he is.'

'Waiting,' she said. 'What are we going to do?'

'We can't stay here.'

For some reason the room with the destroyed

eagle and the sour smell and dust seemed to hold a far greater terror than the hall outside with the stealthy creak of floorboards.

'I have the gun,' I said.

'Do you think you can use it?'

'I—I think so. Put out the light, Billie.'

'But, Em—'

'We'll be safer if he can't see us.'

She blew out the lamp, set it down in darkness. I opened the door. The hinges creaked loudly, a grating noise that split the silence. The sound echoed in the hall, died down, vanished, and there was nothing but the soft sound of breathing and the gentle rustle of the curtains billowing in the now light breeze. I reached for Billie's hand and squeezed it. We were both acutely aware of the danger and acutely aware of the necessity of remaining calm. We crept out into the hall and were soon swallowed up by the shadowy darkness.

We moved towards the staircase, slowly, silently. At each end of the long hall there were pools of light where silver moonbeams drifted through the opened windows, and in between there was darkness, grey at the edges, growing denser, impenetrable in the middle where we moved. It would be impossible to see anyone leaning against the wall, but I could *feel* someone, a presence, a curious current in the atmosphere. I listened for the sound of laboured breathing, the sound of footsteps, but there were no noises. I could not be sure that someone was actually watching us, but I seemed to feel eyes on us as we moved down the hall.

I stumbled against the bannister of the staircase. Billie jerked my hand. I reached out in space and found the railing, ran my palm over the smooth mahogany and began to go down the stairs, Billie following me. I moved down, down, hesitating before each step, and each step screamed in protest, though the noises were actually small squeaks. I knew the noise would bring him screaming out of the shadows and hurtling down the stairs with the axe waving and lusty for blood, but we were halfway down now, and I could see the hazy grey-black of the lower hall. The stairs curled around and there were just a few more to go. I felt the evil behind me, up there, and I tilted my head back and peered. Two hands were gripping the bannister, a torso was leaning over, a face looking down. I could hear breathing, heavy, carefully controlled, spilling down into the stairwell.

Billie heard it, too. She looked up.

We stumbled down the last steps and into the lower hall. We hurried towards the front door, heedless of noise now. It was locked. I fumbled with the bolts, rattled the latch, jerked the heavy brass knob. The door swung open. A flood of silver moonlight swept over the porch and illuminated the hall. We stepped over the dark boards and started to run down the steps. We stopped. We stared at the scene before us. We both forgot the man leaning over the stairwell inside.

Doctor Clarkson's battered blue car was parked crazily in front of the house, both front doors wide open, the headlights mote-filled yellow wands pointing towards the gravelled drive. Doctor Clarkson was sprawled out on the ground midway between the car and the porch, his arms flung out wildly, his head turned to one side. He was still, very still, and something dark and wet covered his forehead and temple. The breeze that drifted from over the water was icy cold, and there was a total silence unbroken by even the hum of insects. I had the feeling that time had stopped dead still.

We must have paused for only an instant, but it seemed like we stood there for an eternity, watching the motes of dust swirling in the wavering headlights, watching the dark wetness spread and slowly drip from his head. I thought, *they've failed me. They promised someone would be watching the house at all times, day and night, and they've failed me. They promised nothing would happen, yet this has happened. Where are they? Why did they let this happen?*

Billie moved before I did. She stepped quickly down the steps and kneeled at his side. She touched his head. She lifted his wrist and felt his pulse. I followed her, numb, shocked. I could see his chest rising and falling, and I could hear his breathing.

Thank God for that, I said silently.

'He's alive,' Billie said in a flat voice. 'He's been hit over the head. There's a lot of blood, but the gash isn't deep. The blood is still warm. He hasn't been here long. What shall we do, Em?'

I was lost, trapped in a nightmare world, too numb to feel, too numb to answer her question. Billie looked up at me and then, after a moment, asked the question again. A tremor went through my body. I came alive and with the feeling of life came decision.

'We can't leave him here,' I said. 'We have to get him to a hospital right away. See if the keys are still in his car.'

Billie looked in the car.

'They're gone,' she said.

'Perhaps they're in his pocket.'

I knelt down and slipped my hand into the doctor's pockets. The keys were not there.

They were not in the ignition. They were not in his pockets. Someone had taken them, deliberately. Coldly, methodically, someone had thought this out. Doctor Clarkson would not likely be needing the keys for a long time, but his assailant knew that we might try to use the doctor's car for escape. I felt an icy chill as I realized this. He knew we would try to get the doctor in the car and get away, and he had made it impossible, and he knew we would not, could not run away and leave the doctor in a critical condition. We were stranded. He had planned it, down to the last detail.

'Em, we can't leave him here alone,' Billie said, her voice firm.

'I know. He knows it, too. That's why he didn't kill the doctor. He could have, but he didn't—because he wanted to keep us here. We could leave a—a corpse, but we couldn't leave an unconscious man.'

'Em—'

'George,' I said. 'George Reed. Go to his cottage. Take the jewels. If he's there, tell him what's happened. If not, he has a telephone, phone the police, tell them.'

'I won't leave you, Em.'

'Don't argue, Billie. Please.'

'What are you going to do?'

'I'm going to get Clive's car and bring it

around here and try to get the doctor in it and—'

'You'll need help for that,' she protested, interrupting me.

'I'll manage.'

'Em, *he's* in there. You can't—'

'Billie, *please*. Go. Get help. Send them. Quickly.'

She searched my face I don't know what she saw there. She started to say something and then checked herself. She touched my arm and started towards the beach, moving lightly, quickly, soon disappearing into the shadows. I stepped over to the car and switched off the headlights. The yellow wands vanished abruptly. I didn't want the lights on me as I walked around the house and down the drive. The night noises returned. I heard a cricket under the steps, heard the wind rustling the grass on the beach and the sea slip softly over the shingles.

I braced myself, trying to summon the courage I knew I would need. *He* was there, and they had failed me. Someone will always be watching after you, George had promised. He had been in the house earlier. I knew that as soon as Billie told me she found cigarette butts and the magazine article about his father, but where was he *now*? Where was Officer

Stevens, and where were the men who were supposed to be watching the house? It will be a perfect trap, George said. Yes, and I would be the bait with my pretended amnesia. The trap was set, a perfect trap, but who was caught? I held the gun gripped tightly in my hand and told myself to stop thinking. Now I must get the car and get the doctor away from this place.

I walked across the lawn and around the front of the house. I did not have my purse, but I knew Clive kept an extra ignition key tucked under the floormat. I would drive away, and nothing would happen. George would come, and the police, and they would capture their criminal and it would all be over. My sandals scraped loudly on the drive. The noise unnerved me. The carriage house was straight ahead, the door yawning open, a black hole. Clouds floated across the moon and shadows drifted across the ground, black and silver and grey. The gravel crunched. My heart pounded.

My God, my God, I thought. What am I doing here? Why did I let them talk me into it? I must have been out of my mind when I said I'd help them do this....

The idea had seemed preposterous at first. I told George that. I said I couldn't possibly pretend to have amnesia. I couldn't fool anyone. George was Doctor Clarkson's protégé... Doctor Clarkson helped send him to medical school, and he would help with this, too. So would Officer Stevens, Burt Reed's drinking buddy and lifetime friend who didn't believe for a minute that old Reed had murdered Henrietta. The three of them worked out all the details. Officer Stevens knew about the will and knew I would inherit the house and have a logical reason for coming back. Doctor Clarkson brought me books on amnesia and discussed them with me. George saw to it that everyone knew I had 'witnessed' the crime and been shocked into amnesia. It was all smooth, all simple. Although George had come to London several times, we had seen each other in secrecy, and none of my friends knew of my engagement, not even Billie, nor had I ever talked of Henrietta or the months in Brighton.

I had been in London the night Henrietta was murdered. When they told me about it I was desolate, but there was nothing I could do. I didn't go to her funeral. I sent her favourite roses and grieved in my own way, and this fit in perfectly with the plan, for if I had appeared at the funeral when I was supposed to have been 'in the hospital,' the whole fabric of the deception would have fallen through. I wanted to help. They were all three convinced of Burt Reed's innocence, but the case had been closed, and the only way they could prove he didn't do it was to find out who did. I agreed to help, because I loved George, because I felt I owed it to Henrietta.

At the last minute I tried to back down. I didn't have the courage to go through with it. I couldn't come to the house alone and stay here, not for George not for Henrietta, not for anyone, and then Billie said she wanted to come with me. I couldn't do it. I couldn't expose her to danger, too. But there would be no danger, they insisted. Someone would be there watching, waiting for the killer to show himself. Billie mustn't know anything about it, because she might say something, accidently of course, but nevertheless she might let on. We couldn't risk that. She was coming to help find a killer.

We came. The trap was set.

I almost gave it away when Nelson came running across the lawn and put his head in my lap, and George overplayed terribly, first for Billie's benefit, later for Boyd Devlon. And later on, in the kitchen, I entirely forgot my role and started preparing dinner with all the assurance of one completely familiar with the room and its cabinets and drawers. Boyd noticed that, and I covered up as well as I could, saying I had explored the room earlier. It had been hard from the very first, and I had to pretend even to myself that everything, so deeply felt, so well remembered, was strange and new.

Now there was no need for pretence. Now I knew who had murdered Henrietta. I moved slowly towards the carriage house, tense, terrified, holding the gun tightly in my hand.

I could see Clive's car in the darkness of the garage. Just a few more yards. Keep calm. Stay cool. Don't break, not now, not when everything is almost over. Get the car. Drive it around front. Help the doctor. Be very brave. I moved towards that nest of darkness, and when I was almost at the great open door the shadows seemed to melt and Boyd Devlon moved out of them, stepping quietly out onto the drive and blocking my way. My heart leaped. My throat went dry.

He didn't say anything. He stood there with his hands resting lightly on his thighs, a curious smile on his wide lips. His hair spilled over his forehead in unruly waves. His eyes were full of mockery. I stopped, three yards away from him. I closed my eyes. I whispered a silent prayer. I tried with all my might to force back the hysteria that rose up in panic-stricken waves to engulf me. I managed to maintain a shaky control, and I held the gun out with trembling hand and stared at him over the short black barrel.

'Are you going to shoot me?' he inquired casually.

'If I have to,' I said.

'Why should you want to do a thing like that?'

'You know very well.'

'Tell me,' he said, still smiling.

'You murdered Henrietta.'

'Come now, Emmalynn—'

'It's all in her diary, Boyd. Everything.'

'Diary?' He looked bewildered.

'I know who you are. I know why you came here. I know why you stayed on even after you'd killed her and framed Burt Reed.'

'And why did I?' He asked quietly.

'You wanted the jewels. You knew she had them hidden somewhere in the house, but you couldn't find them. Gordon Stuart wanted them, too, but he didn't want them enough to kill for them. I was certain he'd done it. He was capable of such a crime, and he had a strong motive, but not as strong as yours.'

The smile was still flickering on his lips, but I could see that he was growing uneasy, restless. He dug the toe of his shoe in the gravel. His strong hands curled into fists, and he lowered his eyelids, staring at me through narrow slits.

'You murdered your mother,' I said.

'Did I?'

'Don't try to deny it, Boyd.'

'I see you've regained your memory,' he said.

'I never lost it.'

He nodded his head briefly. 'I see. Oh yes, I see now. I knew you were carrying on with Reed, but I thought—I really believed—you'd forgotten it.'

I made no comment. I held the gun firmly.

'When I saw you had amnesia, I thought I would get you to throw away everything else and join forces with me. I thought I could convince you we had been lovers. But you wouldn't buy that. You *knew* there'd never been anything between us, and you let me go on making a fool of myself. There could have been something though, back then—'

'I was barely aware of your existence,' I said.

'True. You were too wrapped up in George Reed to notice anything. I stayed on here because I assumed you knew where the jewels were, would come back for them. I would bide my time. You would come. You would get the jewels, and I would take them from you. The amnesia bit threw me.'

'It was intended to,' I replied.

'I knew I would have to kill you, Emmalynn. As soon as you began to remember, as soon as I'd forced you to show me the hiding place.'

His eyes grew cloudy, and a deep frown creased his brow. 'She was a sly old bitch. She knew I was after the jewels and she kept hiding them in different spots to confuse me. After I killed her I thought for sure I'd find them. I've searched every room in this house, over and over again. I knew they were here.'

'Last night,' I said. 'You were in her room.'

'You almost caught me. I was just coming out when you stepped into the hall and went to her room. I hung around, thinking maybe you'd remembered and would find the jewels, even though I'd just gone through the room with a knife, looking everywhere. You didn't even *know* about the jewels.'

'Not until today,' I told him.

'You came here to trap me.'

'Exactly,' I said. 'And I have,' I added, pointing the gun at his chest. I was in complete control of myself now. I had the gun, and I knew I could use it, would use it if necessary. The corners of his lips curled up, and gave a soft chuckle, not at all intimidated by the short black instrument in my hand.

'So you know,' he said.

'I know. Everything.'

'I never knew who my father was,' he said. 'I wonder if she did? She didn't have the guts to abort me, so she went to Switzerland and gave birth to me, and then left me in Devon with a former maid. They told me all about her. She sent money every now and then, occasionally a Christmas gift, and she even financed my college education, what there was of it, but she would have nothing else to do with me. I knocked around the world, a bastard in every sense of the word, and I vowed that someday I'd get what was rightfully mine. I kept track of my mother, and when she came here I followed her. She was very generous. She gave me a job. She let me put on a uniform and drive her around. She let me sleep over the garage, and sometimes she even gave me a few extra dollars when I wanted to go to town. Oh yes, she was very generous.'

He paused, his face a mask of hatred. There was nothing handsome about Boyd Devlon now. He was like an animal, tense and vicious, holding back, restraining the hot animal rage erupting inside of him. He drove his fist into the palm of his hand. He heaved his shoulders. He took a deep breath and relaxed and stared at me with a controlled, level gaze.

'I killed her,' he said. 'I warned her I would. I told her I'd do it if she didn't at least give me enough to get out of the country and make a new start somewhere. She laughed at me. Mocked me. I stole Reed's axe. I waited until dark and knocked on the door, and when she opened it I let her get a good look at me, a good look at the axe, and then I did it. I hid the axe behind Reed's place and went to Brighton and drank with my buddies, and later I found her body and phoned the police and Reed was arrested. He died in jail and the case was dropped and there were legal difficulties and I stayed on here as caretaker, waiting for you.'

He frowned. 'That damn kid hung around a lot. I chased her away. She was a nosy little thing, and once when I caught her she made a face at me and said she knew something I didn't know and hinted about the murder, and then this afternoon when I was waiting for you at the store she went up to Gordon Stuart and showed him a wooden dog and said Reed had given it to her and he was supposed to be a murderer but she knew for sure he wasn't. So I brought you back here and left again immediately. I saw her on a pier talking with George Reed. He left. I waited. She started walking along the beach. I followed her. I called her. She ran. I trapped her in a hut and killed her.'

'You didn't,' I said. 'You hit her. You merely knocked her unconscious. She's alive, in the hospital.'

He looked stunned.

'She'll talk,' I told him. 'The doctor says she'll be able to talk in two days.'

'Doesn't matter,' he said. 'By then I'll be long gone.'

'No, Boyd.'

'Who's to stop me?'

'You seem to have forgotten about this gun.'

'No,' he said. 'I haven't. I'm very thoughtful, Emmalynn, and very careful. When you and your friend left the kitchen I came back in and unloaded the gun.'

'I don't believe you.'

'Try it,' he said.

I remembered then that I had left the gun on the drainboard, and Billie had found it on the high stool beside the stove. I pulled the trigger. The hammer clicked loudly on metal, but there was no explosion. Boyd smiled a crooked smile and blew breath between his lips. His eyes were full of anticipation and my blood ran cold as I realized what he was anticipating. He took a step towards me, his face chiselled in moonlight and shadow.

'Where are the jewels?' he asked. His voice was throaty.

'Gone,' I said.

'Gone? They're here, hidden. You know where they are.'

'Billie took them. She left.'

'You're lying.'

'They were in the eagle. We found them there. You—you saw us leaving the room. We had the pouch—'

He stared at me, bewildered, confused, a heavy crease in his brow. He realized then that I was telling the truth. He realized the jewels were gone. His face fell. It seemed to crumple. I thought for a moment he was going to cry. He clenched and unclenched his fists and made a strange noise in his throat. He looked up at me finally, and his eyes were glazed. Without a word he turned and stepped into the garage. I saw him bend down to pick something up. I watched, paralysed, held rooted to the spot with a horrified fascination.

He came out of the garage with a heavy wrench. It was long and black, deadly. He held it up by the handle and caressed it with his other hand. I saw that the end was wet with blood and knew that this was what he had used to hit Doctor Clarkson. Boyd caressed the wrench and moaned, a sound like crooning. He stood with his legs wide spread, his shoulders hunched forward, his powerful body silver in moonlight, his grotesque shadow black and distorted against the drive.

I knew that this man was insane. I knew that he intended to kill me. I tried to scream, but no sound would come out. I wanted to run, but my feet were glued to the drive and my whole body was frozen with a terror that was like a physical force holding me down.

Boyd looked down at the wrench and studied it as though it were an object of great beauty. He crooned softly, the most terrifying noise I have ever heard issue from a human throat, and then he looked up at me, and I saw the face that Henrietta must have seen in her last moment of life. It was not a human face. It was a face with all humanity crushed aside by the madness that possessed the man. He raised the wrench, and he giggled. He came towards me, moving slowly, each step crunching loudly on the drive. I saw the arm with the wrench raise back, saw him tense for the blow, heard him giggle again.

Then the explosion came.

I was in the centre of the explosion. Gravel flew. Voices yelled. I felt arms flung about my body. I was thrown to the ground. I saw a streak of orange flame, heard another explosion and a shrill piercing scream and I looked up to see Boyd Devlon with his mouth hanging open, his eyes wide, a circle of scarlet spreading on his forehead. For an instant he stood there with his body still tensed for the blow, the wrench raised high, and then he fell with an enormous thud of dead weight. Men ran around, scattering gravel. I glimpsed Officer Stevens. I saw uniforms and boots. I felt the arms still around me, and my body was throbbing with pain from the tackle. George and I were both in the middle of the drive, surrounded by a chaos of noise and confusion.

He touched my chin with his fingers, and his face was incredibly tender. His dark brown eyes were full of concern, but his mouth was smiling. He ran his fingers over my lips, my cheeks, touched my eyelids as though they were exquisitely fragile.

'I was with you every minute,' he said, his voice husky.

'Upstairs—in the hall—'

'Me,' he said, 'watching you.'

'The police—'

'The house was surrounded with them, one behind every tree. They saw him attack the doctor, but he disappeared into the garage before they could get him. Stevens decided to wait until you came out. We wanted to hear him confess—we weren't ten feet away from you—'

'Why did—'

He laid his hand over my lips. He cradled me in his arms there on the ground, amidst of all the chaos and shouting. 'Later,' he whispered, and I laid my head against his chest and tried to forget.

CHAPTER SIXTEEN

The hotel was one of Brighton's finest, and our room was large and airy and dazzling with sunlight pouring through the French windows that opened onto a terrace overlooking the sea. We had been here for almost a week now, and Billie had already obtained a gorgeous tan and the fawning admiration of an equally gorgeous pop singer from Liverpool who had rugged features and soul blue eyes and dark brown hair Samson would have envied. He had seen her on the beach in her bikini and had been promptly smitten. In just a few days he was leaving for America to appear on television and make a record album and become an overnight celebrity, and he wanted to spend all his time with Billie before the plane carried him across the ocean.

Billie sat at the mirror and ran her fingers through her hair until it was suitably disarrayed and then smoothed a final touch of brown shadow on her eyelids.

'Imagine my horror,' she said, 'leaving you there and knowing Devlon was lurking around and finding George's cottage locked and having to break a window to get in and then phoning the police and being told they were already gone—'

'You were very brave,' I told her.

'You were magnificent,' she replied.

'Just frightened,' I said.

'I still think you should go on the stage,' she said, standing up and smoothing the skirt of a leaf brown shift whose exquisitely simple lines had been tailored by Quant. 'You had me fooled from the word go,' she said. 'I had no *idea* you were faking it. You've missed your calling. J Arthur Rank could use you. Just the same, I don't see why you couldn't have given a hint.'

'I had my reasons,' I said.

'I understand. I might have let something slip, though actually I'm quite trustworthy. Anyway, I wouldn't have missed it for the world. It's been enchanting. We'll be the centre of attention at all the London parties for months—unless I decide to go to America.'

'You think that's possible?'

'*Anything* is possible,' she said.

She yawned slightly, looking appropriately

bored, but I could tell she was filled with zestful vitality that no amount of high fashion could conceal. This same blasé Billie had spent half the afternoon at the hospital, reading aloud to Betty and managing to subdue and delight the child who had already driven two nurses berserk and threatened to tear the whole hospital down if she wasn't released soon.

'Did Evans come today?' Billie asked.

'Yes. He came this afternoon while you were at the hospital.'

'And?'

'And I signed the final papers and the house belongs to him now and I feel like a thief for taking all that money for it.'

'Don't,' she said. 'He'll make a fortune.'

'You think so?'

'I'm certain.'

Doctor Clarkson, looking rakish with a bandage on his head, had introduced me to Roderick Evans three days ago. Evans had a long, pale face and sleek black hair and looked as though he'd been reared in Dracula's castle. He was the location man for a film company who made grade C horror movies and millions of dollars each year, and he wanted to capitalize on the publicity the Stern place had received. The house would be used as the setting for a movie and then turned into a tourist attraction. Evans believed the insatiable and morbid curiosity of the general public would make the place a national landmark and that guided tours at a dollar a head would make him a millionaire. The idea repelled me at first. Then I realized it was exactly the kind of thing that would have delighted Henrietta, and I agreed to sell.

Billie glanced at the clock.

'It's almost six,' she said. 'Rufus will be ringing for me any minute now.'

'Dinner?' I inquired.

'Of sorts. A jazz session at one of the clubs with the combo he sings with and then a party given by a rich, rich matron who has a crush on the drummer and, if we're lucky, a short cruise on her husband's yacht.'

'Glamorous,' I said.

'Very. Is George taking you out?'

I nodded. 'He's taking me to the movies.'

'The movies!'

'Jeanne Moreau at one of the art houses. She's the only woman on earth I'm jealous of. George never misses one of her films.'

'Have a jolly time,' she said.

'I will. He'll buy me a bag of popcorn and tell me to keep quiet, and after the movie he'll talk about that marvellous face for several hours and ask me how many times I saw *Jules et Jim*.'

'Sounds like fun.'

'I envy you your yacht,' I said.

'And I envy you your George.'

The doorbell rang. Billie picked up the dark green leather purse that matched her square-toed shoes and went to open the door. Rufus Mann came in and devoured her with the magnificent blue eyes and stuck his thumbs in the wide brown leather belt that kept his bell-bottomed tan trousers from slipping off his narrow hips. He wore a dark yellow Tom Jones shirt with enormous full-gathered sleeves. Billie nodded at him and stifled another yawn. She reminded me of a spoiled child being pacified with a shiny new toy, but I knew her lack of enthusiasm was only the expected pose. They left, and I started thinking of rugged pop singers with spectacular futures and decided I preferred medical students whose futures were more solid.

Thirty minutes later I was downstairs in the large, elegant green and white lobby, waiting for George. I stood by one of the columns, my hair a shining auburn cap. I was wearing a beige silk dress and feeling very feminine and attractive. This was to be my last night in Brighton and I wanted it to be special, even though we were only going to the movies. I watched plump middle-aged matrons in black and grey giving imperious orders to bellboys in dark brown uniforms and I saw a florist walk through the lobby with an immense bouquet, and I thought she must be lucky indeed to have a man thoughtful enough to send them.

The large clock on the wall told me that George was already five minutes late. I tapped the toe of my shoe on the polished marble floor.

Another five minutes passed. The theatre was half a mile away, and the feature would be starting soon. I frowned slightly, accustomed to waiting for George and not really minding at all. He was always worth the wait. I glanced at the rack of newspapers near the front desk. The headlines still blazed details of the Stern case, although five nights had passed since Officer Stevens had been forced to shoot Boyd Devlon. Details of that night came back to me as I waited.

There had been men posted in the woods that surrounded the house since the moment Billie and I arrived in Brighton, and they remained there night and day, waiting, watching, always concealed. Although George had given a good show of staying at his own cottage, he had been inside the house both nights we were there, stationed in a room within calling distance of my own and watching over us at all times. I told him it would have saved me a lot of worry if I had *known* he was there, and he heaved his shoulders and gave me a manly look and said he hadn't wanted to alarm me. That exasperated me. I could have shot him on the spot.

All the men were on the alert for someone prowling around, trying to break into the house. Boyd Devlon belonged. He had a legitimate reason for being there, and they had paid little attention to him until it was almost too late.

He had been on the front porch when Doctor Clarkson drove up. He went towards the car casually, as though to greet the doctor, then pulled him out and hit him and disappeared into the garage before Officer Stevens or any of his men could reach him. Stevens had checked to see that the doctor was not seriously injured and then shrewdly decided to wait before sending his men after Devlon. He needed to hear the whole story from Devlon's own lips, and the only way he could do that was to follow the original plan and let me draw it out of him. When I came out and sent Billie away and started towards the carriage house, the men moved with me, stepping noiselessly on the grass and staying in the shadows. I was as unaware of their presence as Boyd had been.

When Boyd raised the wrench to hit me with it, George flew through the darkness and tackled me and the police charged Boyd, yelling at him, warning him to drop the wrench. He drew the wrench back and was about to hurl it when Officer Stevens shot him. Death was merciful for Boyd. He had been hopelessly insane, and death was preferable to the life he would have had to live had it not been necessary to shoot him. I remembered that look on his face as he started towards me with the wrench. I remembered the giggle. Those were things I would never be able to forget.

The newspapers had exploded with the story, filling column after column with details that sparkled with journalistic fireworks. They did not carry the full story. It remained a secret to all but a few people. Boyd's relationship to Henrietta was not revealed, and my own name was mentioned only in passing, thanks to Officer Stevens' influence with the press. The stories merely said that I had inherited the house and came back to inspect it and was there when Devlon went berserk, attacked the doctor and was shot by the police. The tabloids made a regular heroine of Betty Murphy who had had a remarkably rapid recovery and summoned the reporters herself, calling them on the sly from the phone in her hospital room. Doctor Martin, who was in charge of the patient, noted the colour in her cheeks and the excitement in her voice and agreed to let her relish her glory.

With her scabby knees and scratched cheeks, her arm in a cast and her shaggy blonde hair in her eyes, she held court like a raucous young princess, demanding full attention, brazenly exaggerating, shamelessly refusing to give pertinent details unless she was 'properly treated.' I had been to see her earlier today, and her room had been filled to overflowing with stuffed toys, books, flowers, boxes of candy and other fruits of her blackmail. For three days she had been the darling of the press, and today she had been rather sulky because her picture wasn't on the front page of the morning news.

A less sensational story had appeared in the papers day before yesterday. Gordon Stuart had been arrested for fraud and embezzlement and was in jail awaiting trial. He had been unable to raise bail money. Doctor Clarkson, always informed, told me that Gordon's business associates had discovered the loss of the money Gordon had 'borrowed' and pressed charges immediately. I felt rather sorry for Gordon. His schemes and plans had finally caught up with him, and he was buried under the rubble after they had collapsed on him.

I was lost in thought when George came into the lobby. For a moment I didn't see him. When I glanced up he was ambling towards me, looking ill at ease in the elegant surroundings. He wore a rumpled brown suit that fit too tightly across the shoulders and a perfectly hideous red and brown tie that was poorly knotted. His hair was brushed severely to one side of his head, and there was a preoccupied look on his broad, unhandsome face. I was very proud of him, despite the horrible clothes, despite the lack of ease. Men like George Reed are created to dig canals and build skyscrapers and do wonderful things in medical science. They are not made to look appealing or to adorn society.

I thought he looked very appealing.

He was approximately four yards from me before he recognized me. The heavy horn-rimmed glasses were effective only when he happened to remember to look through them. Much of the time his mind was far away. He stopped short and jammed his hands in his pockets and grinned at me when he finally noticed me standing by the column.

'Hey,' he said.

For a moment I thought he was going to comment on the new dress. I was wrong, of course.

'You ready?' he asked.

'I don't know,' I said, rather nastily.

'Huh?'

'I said I don't know.'

'Well for crying out loud—why not?'

'I don't think I want to go to the movies.'

'Have you lost your senses?'

'No. I think I've just *come* to them.'

George scowled. He shrugged his shoulders. He gripped me by the elbow and ushered me out of the hotel before I could protest. The sun was going down, staining the horizon with gold and orange streamers, and the broad Esplanade with its fine hotels and exquisite shops took on a hazy beauty in the fading light. The sea was majestic now, the water dark blue, the waves gentle as they washed over the carefully kept beaches. George was leading me towards his car, an ancient Ford with a bashed front fender and a shattered rear windshield. One door had been painted black after an accident had removed the original paint. It was a ghastly sight parked there beside a gleaming Cadillac and a wickedly beautiful black Mercedes.

I planted my heels firmly on the concrete and refused to move one more step.

'What *is* this?' George protested, completely bewildered.

'Did you know I own a Rolls Royce?' I said angrily.

'Large deal. So?'

'I don't *have* to ride in that wreck.'

'I don't understand—'

'I am an heiress. I have a fortune in jewels alone.'

'Sure you do. So what the hell?'

'Billie's got a date with a pop singer from Liverpool.'

'I bet he has long hair and beads.' George said, which was maddening.

'He's perfectly marvellous.'

'And?'

'And on my last night in Brighton I don't see why I should go to the movies and spend the rest of the evening listening to you rave about Jeanne Moreau and treat me like an old shoe you just happened to find somewhere.'

'Who said anything about movies?' he said. 'You think I dressed up like this to go to the movies?'

'You said last night you wanted to see—'

'But I phoned you—'

'You did *not* phone me,' I said, emphatic.

'I intended to,' he said, sheepish.

'That's what I *mean*, George. You always intend.'

'I intended to call you and tell you I talked to Doctor Goldberg who's head of the school and he said Doctor Clarkson had already made all the arrangements for me to finish the work I need for my degree and that we were going to go out on the town tonight and celebrate and

I was going to drive you back to London myself in the morning and then start looking for a flat near the hospital and you could keep working for that crazy photographer until I finish doing my internship and then—'

I listened in stony silence. George looked menacing.

'Didn't you get the roses?' he barked.

'I most certainly did not.'

'I know damn well I sent three dozen roses.'

'Yellow roses?' I asked, subdued.

'I *told* the man yellow!'

'My favourite kind,' I whispered.

'Look, you wanna go or not?'

'What do you think?'

'I don't think you have any choice,' he said firmly.

He was right. He usually is.

The publishers hope that this book has given you enjoyable reading. Large Print Books are especially designed to be as easy to see and hold as possible. If you wish a complete list of our books, please ask at your local library or write directly to: Magna Print Books, Long Preston, North Yorkshire, BD23 4ND England.